NO LAND
TO
LIGHT
ON

NO LAND TO LIGHT ON

a novel

YARA ZGHEIB

ATRIA BOOKS

New York   London   Toronto   Sydney   New Delhi

ATRIA
BOOKS

An Imprint of Simon & Schuster, Inc.
1230 Avenue of the Americas
New York, NY 10020

Copyright © 2022 by Yara Zgheib

All rights reserved, including the right to reproduce this book or portions thereof in any form whatsoever. For information, address Atria Books Subsidiary Rights Department, 1230 Avenue of the Americas, New York, NY 10020.

First Atria Books hardcover edition January 2022

ATRIA BOOKS and colophon are trademarks of Simon & Schuster, Inc.

For information about special discounts for bulk purchases, please contact Simon & Schuster Special Sales at 1-866-506-1949 or business@simonandschuster.com.

The Simon & Schuster Speakers Bureau can bring authors to your live event. For more information or to book an event, contact the Simon & Schuster Speakers Bureau at 1-866-248-3049 or visit our website at www.simonspeakers.com.

Interior design by Jill Putorti

Manufactured in the United States of America

1 3 5 7 9 10 8 6 4 2

Library of Congress Cataloging-in-Publication Data
Names: Zgheib, Yara, author.
Title: No land to light on / Yara Zgheib.
Description: First Atria Books hardcover edition. | New York : Atria, 2022.
Identifiers: LCCN 2021019894 | ISBN 9781982187422 (hardcover) | ISBN 9781982187439 (paperback) | ISBN 9781982187446 (ebook)
Subjects: LCSH: Newlyweds—Fiction. | Syrians—United States—Fiction. | Refugees—Syria—Fiction. | Travel restrictions—Fiction. | GSAFD: Love stories. | LCGFT: Novels.
Classification: LCC PS3626.G44 N6 2022 | DDC 813/.6—dc23
LC record available at https://lccn.loc.gov/2021019894

ISBN 978-1-9821-8742-2
ISBN 978-1-9821-8744-6 (ebook)

For Camille and Michaël

With no land to light on,
they look back without nostalgia,
and look forward with a frayed hope.

—MICHAEL ONDAATJE

Sama," she said and he heard, though she said it lightly. It rang, clear, across an oak room in Massachusetts, over effervescing champagnes and violins, over the sea of dark suits. He turned and saw a white chiffon dress.

A pause on a melody, quarter note rest. The piano he left in Douma, the sheets inside the bench. He held his breath, afraid that if he exhaled, he would wake up. She took a sip from a long-stemmed flute rimmed with fine etchings that caught chinks of light.

"It means sky in Arabic."

2011

Pro-democracy protests erupt in Syria, demanding the end of the authoritarian practices of the Assad regime, in place since 1971. The Syrian government uses violence to suppress the demonstrations. Opposition militias form.

2012

The Syrian uprising escalates into civil war.

2015

By the end of the fifth year of violence, the number of Syrian refugees reaches 4.27 million, according to the UN High Commissioner for Refugees. Of those, the United States pledges to resettle ten thousand within the year.

Poised on the split second between light and dark, a flock of red knots—thousands upon thousands of sandpipers—fills the sky above forty miles of shore and dunes in Cape Cod, Massachusetts. The birds are the color of the setting sun, so small, so frighteningly light, their bones thin as soda straws, and flimsier.

They stop to rest and refuel before resuming their 15,000-kilometer journey across the planet. These little birds are on their way from the Arctic to Tierra del Fuego, a feat as unimaginable as a paper plane reaching the moon.

January 27, 2017

EXECUTIVE ORDER 13769
PROTECTING THE NATION FROM FOREIGN
TERRORIST ENTRY INTO THE UNITED STATES

By the authority vested in me as President . . .

5(c) . . . I hereby proclaim that the entry of nationals of Syria as refugees is detrimental to the interests of the United States and thus suspend any such entry until such time as I have determined . . .

. . . The sky is studded with stars, timeless and infinite. On the shore, there aren't enough crab eggs to feed the red knots. The decline of horseshoe crabs, due to hunting and land degradation, has caused more than 70 percent of red knots to disappear. The birds still go, but each year, fewer and fewer alight in Massachusetts.

January 28, 2017

SAMA

It is much too hot in here. Only my hands are freezing, even as they sweat onto the railing. *Come on, Hadi, call.*

So loud in this airport. Someone is shouting. More join in. I wish they would stop, that they would stop pushing. Officers and dogs. Angry protesters. Discombobulated chanting. Something is going on, but I don't have the strength, or the space, to turn around. I just want to sit down. My feet won't hold my weight, and the baby's, much longer. I contemplate dropping to the floor. If I do, I'll never get up. I think of the old woman I saw trip at a demonstration once.

The stampede crushed her fingers. How she screamed. This isn't Syria, this isn't Syria. People don't get crushed in Boston. People don't get crushed by frantic mobs at Logan Airport.

A heavy woman—her shirt is soaked—pushes me from behind, digging into my back, shoving me into the railing. A cramp. Too mild a word. A punch to my abdomen. I wish I could tell her to stop. I wish you were here; you would. But she knocked the air out of me, and you are somewhere beyond Arrivals. Another shove, cramp, like hot pliers reaching in, squeezing. I shield my stomach with my arm. A cowardly, futile attempt to protect the baby.

The iron rail seeps cold through my sweater, yours, the soft white one you wore the day before you traveled. I told you the stain would come out. I had to roll the sleeves. It doesn't smell of you since I washed it. *Come on, Hadi, call. Please call.*

You should be here. No, we should be home. Your plane landed too long ago. I didn't want to call; it would have ruined the surprise. Now, I don't want to because of the cold, heavy stone in my stomach. And another feeling, higher, like when you miss a step on the stairs, except longer.

The table is set at home. I left the hummus on the counter. A sudden force from behind hurls me into the barrier. My breath bursts out of my lungs. The phone nearly flies out of my hand, lighting up in the same moment.

"Hadi?"

"*Allo?* Sama!"

My breath catches. I know that *Allo*, those soft, gravelly *a*s in my name.

"Hey! Where are you!"

There is much shouting around you too, but in your chaos, unlike mine, one voice thunders over the others, barking words I cannot distinguish.

"Hadi! Can you hear me?"

"Sama?"

2

You cannot. I press my mouth to the phone:

"I'm outside!"

"At the airport? What the hell are you doing here?!"

"I—"

"Are you crazy? Go home!"

"What? No, no, I'm waiting—"

"Sama, I can't come out!"

More shouting on both ends of the line. The shoving behind me. Crescendo. Distinct chanting, pounding: *Let-them-go! Let-them-go!* The ground shakes with their anger.

"What do you mean you can't come out?"

Another blow in my gut. I double over.

"I don't know! No one's told us anything! They took our passports . . . it's . . . What the hell is going on around you?"

"They took your passport?!"

Let-them-in! Let-them-in!

"Sama, the baby!"

I know.

"Is it your travel permit? It can't be!"

"No, they didn't even look at it! Listen—"

But the pounding, this time on your end of the line, drowns the rest.

". . . just go home! I'll figure it out and—"

"Hadi? Are you there?"

Another spasm. My awareness crashes back into Arrivals. The crowd in furious waves. *Let-them-in!* A shove. I lose the phone. The next blow throws me headlong, belly, baby first, to the ground. Instinct buckles my knees; they take the impact.

The mob rages. My memory hears that woman's fingers break, but through blurry patches in my vision, I see the phone and lunge for it. Bursts of fire in my stomach, but I nab it.

Gasps for air and light. I grab someone's jeans.

"Help me, please!"

But my voice is too hoarse, the chorus too loud. I pull, and pull, and pull at those jeans. Then I bite. The foot kicks me in the nose. I yelp but do not let go, crying through my clenched teeth until I am yanked, finally, up, feeling something wet and sticky run down my upper lip. I taste salt.

Surface. White spots of light and cool, cool air.

"Please!"

I sputter, begging the faceless arms that lifted me.

"Please, I'm pregnant!"

The grip tightens. A voice shouts:

"The lady's pregnant! Get out of the way! Get her out of here!"

In lurches, he pulls me, using his back to part the crowd. Every hit is a stab in my gut. I hold on like I am drowning.

"Move out of the way!"

More voices join. More arms drag me out of the raging sea, to the exit. The spots in front of my eyes clear: signs, people waving flags, some wearing them like cloaks and capes. Not all are American. I recognize the Syrian flag: red, white, black, the two green stars. Some have painted it on their cheeks.

"Ma'am!"

Another voice. A uniform.

"Do you need an ambulance?"

I try to speak but another contraction hits. *Too early.* I gasp and nod violently.

"Do you have your ID?"

My purse . . .

"Who are you with?"

Hadi . . .

Gurney. Steely hands, blue gloves. A rotting smell of sweat on rubber. We burst out into the icy air. Ink-black sky, and ahead, blue, white, red lights, wailing like a diabolical arcade game.

Spasm through the ER doors. The blood drains from my face.

Another bang. My fingers grip your sweater, soaked with my sweat, and clench. Every muscle follows, hardened lead. I bite my scream.

"Ma'am, is there someone you can call?"

"My husband!"

"Is he on his way?"

"He doesn't know I'm here!"

Blindly, I wave my phone.

"Hadi. His name is Hadi!"

My voice is chalky. I try again:

"Hadi . . ."

She takes the phone, dials, eyes on me.

"No answer. Is there someone else?"

Whirring, chafing rubber wheels on linoleum. Shouts, but unlike at the airport, these are cold, disjointed.

"Still no answer, ma'am."

The contractions come, too fast. The pain shoots up, down. My feet jerk, teeth crash against one another. My lungs suck shut, cling to my ribs, like I've been plunged into ice water.

"How far along?"

I cannot see the faces. *Twenty-eight weeks*, but there is no air underwater.

"We need to stop the contractions."

"How dilated is she?"

"Seven centimeters."

"Too late. Get an OR ready."

Drowner's reflex.

"No, wait!"

Fire as I force air in.

"My husband is coming!"

Though that cannot be true. You cannot even know I'm here, but maybe if I scream louder.

"Sama."

Someone said my name. Someone said my name.

"Your placenta has ruptured. We need to get this baby out, now, or it will die. Do you understand? Sama?"

Sama Zayat, wife of Hadi Deeb who won't answer his phone, who promised he'd assemble the crib, who promised he'd be back, who promised all would be well, and duty-free Baci chocolates. I nod and shut my eyes against this entire scene.

Now, it isn't happening. I am not in labor and the baby isn't dying. No one took your passport. I misheard, Hadi. You said you forgot to buy the chocolates, or you bought dark, not milk, or left your passport at the register.

Someone found it, found you, and now you will find me. I don't want the chocolates, Hadi. Just come, find me. Let's go home. The hummus will have soured. We'll throw it out. You'll be angry because of the starving people in Syria. I'll feel guilty, but I'll still be pregnant, and it will be all right and we'll just order a pizza. I'll give you my olives, you'll give me your crust. Contraction. I howl.

"The OR is ready!"

Your sweater is ripped away from me, my last proof of You-

and-I. Cold hands strip me naked and slip me into a robe: blue, anonymous.

"Ma'am, give me your arm!"

No one and nothing waits. An IV in my right arm, a name bracelet on my left. The stretcher bangs through more doors. *Boom! Boom!* like bombs. Why were there Syrian flags at Logan Airport? Hadi, why aren't you here?

How careful we had been; no coffee, wine, air travel. How futile now, slamming into the OR, sweating and freezing. I look around for you, frantically, stupidly, knowing you are not there. I look anyway, heart convulsing. Green scrubs. Blue walls. Three round white lights.

Voices and surgical tools dart about. Something cold, a blade. I scream.

My arms flail. Hands hold them down. My legs are strapped in, spread.

"Ma'am, calm down!"

But my screams are all I have left.

"The baby is crowning! You need to push! Hard!"

I push and cry, like that night of raining glass. My ears scream. My eyes are squeezed so tight that around them I feel blood vessels popping.

"Good! Keep pushing, ma'am!"

"I can't!"

"Come on, Sama!"

I push. For you, Hadi. For our son. Pain bursts out of me, but this explosion is fireworks shooting and burning pink and green sulfur, and I keep pushing and crying, and my entire life is this moment. Nothing ever existed outside it.

HADI

No clock, no windows. Must be forty of us in here. The room stinks of breath and sweat. There aren't enough chairs, and politeness ran out hours ago. I sit on the floor.

It smells better down here, of rose water, to my left. An elderly couple. Iranian? Her face is drawn and shaded, like with a blunt pencil. One thin line of dried kohl runs down the cheek I can see, but she sits perfectly straight and looks ahead. Her husband drowses, his head bobbing on her shoulder. That scent, the warid, wafts out of her chador each time she adjusts his head.

What was she making with warid before she boarded the plane? *Riz bi haleeb*. With rose water and orange blossom, like yours. Mama uses hal, but I prefer yours—I'd never tell her. The way steam and aroma seep out of the pot and swell, so the apartment, all weekend, smells of warid. And your clothes, and your hair. And the way you look, all pink, stirring the rice in the milk till it gets so soft and round it will dissolve the instant I put it in my mouth, and you asking me to taste it and me burning my tongue and not caring. I'd eat the whole pot now, if I could. When all this is over, I want riz bi haleeb for days. Samati, I hope you're home.

I hope someone told you what's going on. I wish someone would tell us. I don't know how long we've been here. They took our cell phones, Sama. You must be sick with worry, popping berry antacids. You always take too many. I hope you ate, at least. I know you didn't. You're waiting for me. Please eat, Sama. Please sleep. Think of the baby. I don't know how long we'll be here. My God, I'm so hungry.

The husband moans. His wife apologizes to me, without meeting my gaze. Her voice cracks, and the streak of kohl: *Diabetes. He must eat. His sugar levels, they are . . . down . . .* Yes, Iranian. I give her a piece of gum. Sugar-free, useless, but it is all I have. She bows her head, and when she takes it, her finger brushes my hand, and more *warid.* Pangs in my stomach and chest.

A girl across from me—Sudanese? Ethiopian?—is shaking. She looks your age but nothing like you, dark as you are pale. Her chin trembles like yours when we fight. I should be as scared as she, more, because of my shit, shit Syrian passport. They took it. My papers are in order though. I know that at least. We checked and checked. We went through them together, one by one, before I left: refugee travel permit; permission to travel—I-131 application *and* approval; marriage certificate; driver's license—mine and yours; our lease; my last three pay stubs. *Khara* Syrian passport. *Khara* Syrian war. *Khara 'aleihon,* what's taking so long? I'm so hungry.

I replace the piece of gum in my mouth, rubber now, with another. Pineapple-coconut, for takeoff and landing, you said as you slipped it in my breast pocket. Only you would buy pineapple-coconut gum.

The piña coladas the weekend after we got married. The buffet. The oysters, crab, jumbo shrimp. Blood-orange salmon, pink beef. I'd gorged myself shamelessly, then been so ashamed, and sick. You kept saying it was okay, that I was on my honeymoon. That I could eat as much as I wanted, that *here*, there was food. But you didn't binge. You'd been in America longer, I guess, long enough to forget, or maybe you never stood in the bread lines. You were never in the cells.

It returns now, that hunger that tastes like fear, that came with fear and the cold, wet smell of the basement rooms of Far' Falastin. I couldn't describe that feeling exactly: base, not human fear, until they fed us cow fodder after three days on brine.

Two years. Two whole years between me and that prison. Still the taste resurfaces. I shove another piece of gum in my mouth. It's cold in here too, but dry.

I have three pieces of your gum left, then . . . I will not think of that. I take my mind, instead, back to those three piña colada days. You in the morning, falling back to sleep, rolling out of bed for food. Swimming, eating, drinking, sex again, sunbathing by the pool while, under your hat and parasol, you read Gibran or Thoreau and I pretended to listen.

Then the flight home, to Boston. The first time I said *home, to Boston.* Saying *I live here* to *What is the purpose of your visit?* at Customs and Border Protection.

I live here, and I have a home, a wife, papers to prove it. I said the same thing, exactly, to the officer tonight. I was polite, I promise, Sama, distracted but polite, my mind already on duty-free chocolates, suitcase, cab, fast-forwarding to bed, clean clothes, and my arm over you—

What happened next did not happen. It cannot be real. The officer did not call for backup then wait behind his plastic booth, not looking at me. Then two of them, armed and in black with insignia, did not handcuff me. They did not grab me, each by an arm, push-drag me down a bright hall, ignore me when I asked where we were going or what I had done. They did not speak to each other, over my head, not bothering to whisper: *Where is he from? Fucking Syria, man. Speaks English though.* Then silence.

I tripped and one of them caught me by the collar. I heard it rip, but at least I wasn't choking anymore. They yanked me right back up and pushed me on, into this room. It's been hours.

It never happened. It's too unreal. We've been here so long, and I'm so hungry and exhausted my thoughts must be muddled. I'll have some more gum—

"Hadi Deeb?"

My head jerks up.

I am yanked up and handcuffed again. The piece of gum shoots out of my mouth, barely missing the old woman's foot.

"Where are we going?"

No answer, again.

"Sir, I need to call my wife. She's waiting for me. She's pregnant—"

I trip, over my laces, or someone's backpack, or someone's legs outstretched on the floor. It doesn't matter.

"Pick up your feet!"

A hairline crack through which something like hate flashes out of him, then the uniformed man moves me on, with one hand, gripping my elbow as though all I am is that square bit of bone and skin. His hand is thicker than my arm. His other is by his side, lightly swaying with my passport.

"I can hold my passport myself."

Nothing.

"Sir, can I have my passport back?"

That feeling, that hunger-fear, the most visceral I ever felt, is back. In Far' Falastin, I learned that if I hugged my belly and crouched, I could sometimes muffle it. But now my hands are behind my back.

"I want to speak to a lawyer. I want my passport and my phone. I need to call my wife!"

That sentence had started out so well.

"Sir, I'm going to have to ask you to calm down, or I will have to restrain you."

I'm already handcuffed, stripped of my ID, in a one-way corridor lined with security cameras. But the rising fear is greater. I fight the grip.

"Sir! Calm down!"

His one hand twists my arm and paralyzes me. I go limp to stop the nerve flashes of pain. He does not loosen his grip. *Don't fuck around like that again*, it says and shoves me forward. This time I obey, and tell myself I'm rational, not a coward.

Not scared. *Just a feeling. It's just a feeling*, Mama used to say when I woke up, sweating, shaking from a nightmare. *It will pass.* I believed her; she never lied, I reminded myself, years later, in the cells. *Just a feeling*, I repeat now.

Another room, smaller. No window or clock here either. A swivel chair and a metal stool on either side of a table. I know which seat is mine. I will not sit. The grip on my arm loosens. One of the men remains. The handcuffs stay on.

The officer—same man from the booth? Same black uniform, short sleeves, gold badge, blue insignia, something under the eagle I can't read—shifts his weight around the table like a jellyfish, and sinks onto the swivel chair. It protests. Not muscular. Big. His grip had been misleading. He looks—clear blue eyes—at me as his finger caresses the pistol at his waist, shiny.

The stool sits between us. He does not seem to notice. He turns to my passport, flipping through it like it's a free pamphlet, with a practiced disinterest that, through the fear, begins to irritate me. I wonder if this man has ever left the country. My stomach grumbles. I wonder if he has ever been hungry, really. Ever seen, or smelled, someone die. People shit themselves when they die. Their bowels loosen. Does he know this? They don't on television, so maybe he doesn't.

"So, you're from Syria?"

He asks casually, as though Syria were a college or a town just outside Boston. I envy him for not hearing gunshots and screams when he says it. *Syria*, not *Sooria*. How would he know what *from Syria* means? I wonder whether he has ever had to pull the trigger of that shiny toy pistol of his.

"Oh, is that what it says on there?"

I look at my passport, astonished. His thick neck snaps up. He heard the venom. Now he sees it.

His eyes are tiny beads in a large, round, glistening face. Disinterest has become disdain.

"That's funny," he says, "but not very smart. I would calm down if I were you." He looks pointedly from my arms, behind my back, to his hand, by his pistol. I should shut up, and almost do, but he tosses the passport back on the table so callously . . .

"You have no right to detain me! It's called racial profiling, and it's illegal! I know my rights. I demand—"

His fist pounds the table, once.

"You 'demand' nothing! You have no rights, you—"

His fist, raised again, stops in midair. He puts it down but does not unclench it. His smile does not return.

"Sir, I'm going to ask you, once again, to calm down. Pursuant to Executive Order 13769 I have every right to detain you and ask you as many questions as I want. If you resist again, you will be subdued and incarcerated. Attacking an officer who's just doing his job—"

"Attack? I didn't attack you!"

Now he smiles. His gaze calmly peruses the small room, and my own, in spite of me, follows. This is what he wants.

No cameras. The door is closed.

"Let's try this again," he says, his eyes back on me, his voice almost sultry.

"Where did you fly from? Damascus?"

"Amman."

"What were you doing in Amman?"

I pause.

Baba, rigid and a grayish white, his hands still, as I had never seen them, clasped piously, comically, over his black suit. His neck thick and swollen over the starched collar. That silly tie. That cold blue room.

"My father died. I was taking care of the burial arrangements."

"Your father is Jordanian?" he asks, tone and countenance unchanged.

"No, Syrian."

Now the eyebrow is raised.

"So why was your father in Jordan?"

He hated ties, and that suit. He only had the one, and he only wore it to marry Mama and to funerals. One suit was all a *fallah* needed; his life was in the orchard. He would never have let himself be buried in a suit and tie.

"My parents had an interview at the US Embassy. The one in Syria is closed. I was trying to get them visas—"

"You have refugee status?" he interrupts.

"Yes."

He opens my passport to check anyway.

I try to explain:

"It's called family reunification. I can—"

"Yes, I know, apply on behalf of direct relatives. You had applied for your parents?"

"Yes, as soon as I arrived in the US—"

"When was that?"

"A little more than two years ago."

He looks up.

I say, "That's how long it takes."

I do not go through *what* it takes, the alphanumeric forms, the DNA tests, the fees, the lawyers, the pleading letters, the phone calls. The supporting documents and the tragicomedy of getting them in a country at war. For two years. For nothing. Baba's heart stopped the night before the interview, and Mama missed the appointment.

I do not bother the officer with the details. He is looking at his watch. My pride won't let me ask him for the time, but my stomach, shamelessly, thunders. He hears it and smiles.

"Hungry?"

I curl my lips in so I don't beg for a piece of bread. I've begged before, but I won't, to him. The officer snaps the passport shut. His amusement has passed.

"So you flew all the way to Amman for a burial."

He would never have let himself be buried in a foreign country. He would never have left from the start, but I was so insistent, and Mama so heartbroken after I left . . .

"My mother was alone. I—"

Another smile.

"You're a good son. Where is she now?"

"Back in Syria."

His nod of approval makes me want to hit him. His eyes then narrow, though his tone remains conversational. He says, like the thought just occurred to him:

"ISIS recruits quite a lot of Syrians in Jordan . . ."

The sentence trails but the gaze remains sharp.

"In fact," he adds offhandedly, "I think their biggest training camps are just outside Amman."

My torso jerks forward. My chest heaves.

"I *am* not," I say, jaw so clenched the words barely come out, "a terrorist."

But the look on his face is triumphant; he broke through. Now he prods:

"No, of course not. None of you are . . ."

"I told you my father died! I went there to bury him!"

"Don't raise your voice at me, sir!"

His spittle hits me in the face. It's over.

"I was in the Marines, you know. Served two tours in I-raq."

So he has been out of the country. His eyes shoot rounds at me.

"I've seen men like you. Mobs outside the embassy, shouting 'Death to America!' The next day, I'd see the same men in line, inventing sob stories, trying to get a visa . . ."

"I told you, I'm a refugee! I've never fought a day in my life! Call my case officer!"

The door crashes open behind me.

"What's going on here?!"

The officer jumps up.

"This guy's being belligerent, sir!"

"No, I'm not!" I shout as I spin around. The handcuffs throw me off balance.

The newcomer is older. There is an extra patch on his sleeve. He does not look at me. To the other officer, he says:

"What country?"

"Syria."

He nods.

"He says he's a refugee."

"Of course, they all are. Does he have papers?"

"Yes."

Sir extends his hand. The officer gives him my passport. A cursory glance; a much longer look, no words, between him and the officer. He snaps the blue booklet shut and only then looks at me.

"Sir, we regret to inform you that you are inadmissible to the US."

The words are in English. They must be.

"What?"

"According to Section Three of Executive Order 13769, and based on information discovered during this CBP inspection—"

"Section what? What information? I told him—"

"—you have been denied entry to the US. You have two options—"

"I live here! I have legal status!"

"Your status is no longer valid."

He has remained calm this entire time. His tone has not risen at all. Unperturbed, as though I had thought, not shouted, my protests, he continues:

"As I was saying, you have a choice: You can either leave the US voluntarily—we'll give you a document to sign—or be forcibly deported. If you are, you should know that you will be barred from reentry for five years, if not permanently."

I teeter backward.

"Either way, your deportation officer"—he nods to the man, still standing at attention behind the table—"will make arrangements for your departure on the next scheduled flight."

He turns to the door. My passport is still in his hand.

I want to shout to him to wait. Demand to speak to someone. My case officer, a lawyer! I know my rights. I have the right to—

But he is already out the door. I lunge after him, eyes on the disappearing blue document that is all I have. I forgot the handcuffs. I lose my balance. My chin hits the floor first, the dirty, grimy floor. I taste the tooth first, then the blood.

There is shouting, alarm, boots approaching, arms grabbing me. My head is jerked upward. Something cold presses hard against the back of my neck. I was wrong; it's not a toy pistol.

November 2015

"So, what brings you to America?"

Crash. He had been floating, flying somewhere between his fourth or fifth glass of champagne, in that liminal space between the ground and golden inebriation. He was not drunk, but had not really landed, yet, to the truth: He was in America.

He tore his eyes away from the girl in the white dress, toward the voice.

"I'm Amber. You're from Syria, right? What brings you to America?"

He didn't know, he wanted to tell her. He didn't know what brought him here, to America and this gilded reception, this room shimmering as through a prism, or a dream, or the fizzing glass he held up. He looked around the library.

Oak-paneled walls lined with hundreds, thousands of books. A heady scent of paper, age, leather, pipe tobacco. Chandeliers sprinkling light, and through large—dizzyingly large—windows, moon and stars pouring in more. Hadi Deeb, a guest at Harvard!

Hadi Deeb, Syrian refugee, who, barely a year ago, had been Hadi Deeb, barely alive, Branch 235 detainee. Who, for months

25

in that nonplace of a prison they nicknamed "Falastin"—a vacuum of time and light—had not seen sky. He had seen girls in corners, naked, eyes vacant, emptied, men sleep on tiles caked with their own blood and feces.

But now, these windows! He could see stars! Champagne tasted like stars. As if Far' Falastin, and all of Syria, had never existed.

Five days ago. Had it been only five days since he'd arrived? Was that all it took to end a world? Five days, and five years, and Omar disappearing, and the final blow when the armed men of the *shabiha*, looking for him, had hit his mother.

Wide-eyed Amber was still waiting: What had brought Hadi Deeb to America? The trunk of a car, a steel container at the back of a truck, a tarmac, three flights over seven time zones . . .

"I took a plane," he said, attempting humor. Amber stared. Hadi Deeb was not funny in English.

A clap on his back.

"You're up, son."

My name is Hadi Deeb, and I would like to thank you all for being here. Thank you for inviting me to speak. It is an honor to be with you tonight" was how the speech began, typed on thick paper that now trembled in his hand. Thankfully, behind the podium, no one could see it. And if he kept his eyes on the paper, on the windows at the back, on the sky, on the stars, on the chandeliers, anything else, he would not see them.

"I would like to thank Mr. Jeffries especially. That I am here at all, in America, is thanks to him. Him and the dozens of other lawyers and hundreds of officers at the State Department, the UN High Commissioner for Refugees, and all the other agencies that make it possible for refugees to—"

His voice got caught at this part, every time, snagging on "escape" like barbed wire. The following words then blurred on the page, each time he practiced them. There were only a few lines, innocuously tracing the path that brought him, and all refugees, to America. A few lines, in neat type, well spaced: registration, initial screening, interviews, documentation, cross-checks, medical examinations, clearance for entry, resettlement . . . But every time he tried to read them, the ink stood and swelled like cement, engorged with the agonizing meaning of what the words had signified.

Years of uncertainty and fear, waiting by, fearing the phone. Fearing it if it rang and if it did not. Fearing the walls, the doors, the neighbors on the other side, all open windows. Expecting, every day, to be found out, rounded up by the *shabiha*, and sent back to Far' Falastin: *khayin*, traitor, for conspiring with the Americans.

"—that made it possible for me to be standing on this podium."

No need to bore the audience with details.

"It is their hard work and your generosity, ladies and gentlemen, which have allowed countless Syrians like me to be resettled and start new lives in America. From food and clothing, to accommodation . . ."

The cheerful quilt on the bed in the room the Jeffries family had given him. The borrowed suit he was wearing, sleeves not reaching his wrists, pants too short, shoulders too wide.

Then he read the statistics. Slowly, so as not to make mistakes in English. Then he thanked the audience, again, for their generosity, before calling Mr. Jeffries onstage so he could ask for more of their support. It was the least he could do for him, this speech. He would be honored, he had said.

"I am honored . . ." He wasn't. He felt wrong. ". . . to be here in front of you . . ."

An honorary refugee, elevated on a podium. A podium for having left, survived Syria, when he was no different, better, or worse than the countless others who hadn't.

"My name is Hadi Deeb."

A file with his name had just happened to reach Mr. Jeffries's hands. He could give the audience a list of other names and files that hadn't. With accompanying faces: Omar, Shadi, Ghaith . . .

"Thank you for having me . . ."

In the cell they had shared in the basement of Branch 235, Far' Falastin, Damascus. He could give the audience the cell's dimensions—two meters by one and a half, about the size of a coffin. Shadi had been an architect.

"I am honored . . ."

He wasn't honored. He was just lucky. He was just Hadi Deeb, alive and lucky. Fucking lucky—applause—to be here.

Before coming to America, Hadi Deeb had never flown. He had dreamt of it as a child, as children do, but not since. He had not dreamt at all for years, even before the uprising. And then, the protests, riots, arrests, windowless interrogations . . . How close, he found out, the prison had been to the airport. How easily, finally, lightly, the plane had taken off . . .

He flew across the room.

He almost didn't. He almost lost his nerve. Hadi Deeb and Sama Zayat wouldn't have met. She wouldn't have noticed. Just as the world wouldn't have noticed if he had not left home. If, at the last minute, he hadn't crossed the threshold. Most people don't cross rooms and oceans, embark on journeys with no promise of land to light on.

The girl in the white dress had her back to him, a wisp of light caught in her earring, a dot. A speck of lapis on her ear. The nape of her neck. Translucent. A nonchalant bun. Loose strands of cocoa hair. He heard himself say:

"Excuse me."

Her cheeks were flushed. Her eyes were the color of wild honey. In time he would notice the streaks of olive green.

In a second he would notice the dimple. In two, that when she smiled, the corners of her eyes crinkled. In time, that when she lied, she had to scratch her nose. That she squinted to read menus. That she denied it. That she went to the bathroom to cry. Denied that. That her chin trembled just before. That she covered it, and wasn't afraid of anything but always slept with the light on.

That she left the closets open and that it would drive him mad. Left notes in his coat pockets, in his shoes! That he loved it. That she favored breakfast, and summer, although autumn for the teas and reds. Birds and books and scrambled and black, no sugar. That in the morning her mouth tasted of warm almonds.

But just wild honey, then.

The moment was interrupted by the athletic, ashy blond, in a tuxedo he clearly owned, who had been talking to her.

"Can I help you?" he said. A hint of irritation. A tuxedo that fit, like him, perfectly in this crowd of crisp shirts and mellow voices. Fine hair and milky skin, while the poor, dark Syrian boy . . .

"I . . ."

He struggled to find the words in English and push them out. They stuck to his tongue like a thick, heavy paste. This was new, this bad dream–like feeling of moving underwater, in slow motion.

"You're Sama?" he asked abruptly, with an accent like tar. He sounded like a brute in English. He sounded dumb. A dumb brute in English who should walk away. But then:

"*Btihki 'arabi*," she said and smiled, and his ears rang, the strangest feeling. He realized he had not heard or spoken Arabic since Syria. From across the world, from that other world, the sentence felt warm and translucent. Light, like jet lag lifting. Jet lag he hadn't noticed he had. Something in him reached for the sounds and clung to them. He nodded.

She hesitated a moment, then smiled, and the dimple returned.

"Sama Zayat," she said, extending her hand. He took it and smelled vanilla and apples—somehow, red.

"*Winti?*" he asked, but she gently suggested he speak in English. He grimaced and tried again:

"How long have you been here?"

"Five years."

She spoke with ease.

"Did you come here to study?"

Sama Zayat took a sip of champagne. She had come here to live. She had left Syria, and left Syria behind, with its low ceilings, to see, smell, taste new lands, words, spices, breads, wines. She was mildly tipsy. She had spent the last five years getting drunk on sky and ideas, insatiably, constantly amazed by how much there was. She had come here to become.

She answered that yes, she had come to Harvard to study anthropology. She was writing a dissertation on the parallels between

33

human and avian migratory journeys. She was particularly interested in the work of nineteenth-century ornithologist William Henry Hudson, who observed a pattern of pre-migratory behavior among certain species of birds, remarkably similar . . .

She took a look at him and laughed, and it rippled through him. A few more chocolate wisps of hair escaped her bun.

"It's about birds, and some people. I work with my advisor, and I also teach a few classes. It's required . . ."

And in that moment—that confluence of chance and choice in which lives are changed and about which books are written—Hadi Deeb fell in love with Sama Zayat.

He had never been in love, never made love. He'd fucked Nepalis, Bangladeshi hookers in Saidnaya clubs, once an Iraqi with blue eyes—all insisting he pay up front. He'd fucked like good Syrian boys did, out of frustration, fast, in the dark. "Love" was not a word a man like him used or often heard.

Sama was eternally in love, with everything. If she had not chosen birds, she would have studied art, or literature, geography, or aeronautics. In another life, she would have been a pilot, a cartographer. She loved books about great explorers, adventure, journeys, travel. She had read Verne, Stevenson, Saint-Exupéry, Camus, Hemingway . . . She had left Syria because in Syria that was all she would ever do.

"Did you come from Damascus?"

She had left Damascus because in Damascus she would have married, cooked, and taught English, perhaps, at the local school.

"I left just as the war began. My parents are still there. What about you?"

"Just outside Douma. Baba has an orchard."

Which he loved. He loved the peppery, chocolaty smell of soil, damp with the previous night. He loved working with his hands. In another life, he would have spent his on his father's land, pruning the trees, eating plums, and drinking lemonade in the shade. He loved Syria but had left Syria because in Syria there was a war.

The violins languished in a familiar cadence as the piece, playing in the background, neared its end. Hadi stopped himself:

"Hear that?"

Sama looked at him.

"That *lahn*? How the music, after"—he searched for the words in English—"after it goes and comes and changes, the melody, it always returns to its original . . . *mouftah*. The *iqaa'* . . ."

He looked to her for help. She scrunched her nose.

"Cadence?"

"It's perfect. This is the one called 'going home.' We had a piano at home . . ."

And it hurt to think of, but the melody was so beautiful, they just listened, and it ended and he smiled sheepishly.

"My mother used to play. She taught me a little. I'm not very good . . ."

And Sama Zayat fell in love with Hadi Deeb.

The musicians began to pack and the crowd to thin. She could have said *Thank you, good night* then and walked away. The world wouldn't have noticed; it is full of such encounters on nights with stars and people and almost-moments.

Instead, she said, "I'm hungry. Are you?"

Famished.

A few blocks and ten minutes away, he had four slices of hot pizza, in quick succession, each the size of a quarter of a large pie; each a gorgeous, greasy, cheesy, saucy mess that lived up to every fantasy he had ever had of an American pizza. She had marinara on her chin and a drop on her white dress.

He had hesitated in front of the grimy, shockingly red-and-yellow pizza shop. It was she who had joyfully, in her cocktail dress, dragged him in. Now they sat on counter stools while she sang along to the music.

A dusty nineties album. A bright orange light hung over the smudged counter of enormous, glowing pizzas. On the walls, large vintage posters advertising Naples; a motley display of black-and-white photographs of famous people who had dined there, whom Hadi did not know; banknotes from countries he had never heard of.

He did recognize the songs. The Backstreet Boys had performed the soundtrack of his youth.

"I had such a crush on Nick," Sama said. "I wanted to be one of the Spice Girls."

"Which one?" Hadi asked, hardly daring to think Emma, who had adorned his bedroom wall.

"Emma, of course."

Sama laughed.

"The one who looked the least like the black-haired, scrawny Syrian girl I was!"

He tried to imagine her, black-haired and scrawny, in Syria, walking past him on a Damascene sidewalk, on a Saturday. He couldn't. Just as he couldn't, now, believe that these songs, playing here and now in a Cambridge pizza shop, had ever played in Syria. That it was possible for songs to exist, simultaneously, for different people in different places. People leading vastly different lives at the same time, eating pizza, singing the same songs . . .

The lines were corny, and he realized he'd had them all wrong, laughably wrong, then. Look at him now. Look at where he was.

He was stuffed. The feeling was foreign and welcome. Yes, Syria was far away. In the lull between two songs, heavy with dough and cheese, they slumped onto their seats.

"So, why birds?"

"My dissertation?"

Hadi nodded. He saw her lashes flit and a light flicker on.

"I saw a red knot for the first time when I came to the US. I don't think they exist in our part of the world. The first autumn, a whole skyful of them on their way to Florida. Some people call them sandpipers. They're tiny birds, so tiny one could fit in the palm of your hand. But every year they travel from the Arctic to Tierra del Fuego in Argentina, then back."

"Why?"

"Warmer climates, for one thing. Food, but also . . . it's a mystery. There are nearer destinations, and this journey of theirs . . . Nine thousand miles one way, Hadi! They cross two continents, literally from one end of the earth to the other. If you saw how small they are . . . It's spectacular."

"Spectacular," he echoed, though it sounded more like a question. He still did not understand. She fretted with her napkin.

"It's just wonderful, how free they are, how far they will go to find home . . ."

They were quiet, but after a while she added:

"It's endangered now, the bird."

"Why?"

"Humans. We're destroying the shorelines where they stop to rest, hunting the crabs they eat. These birds have been around tens of thousands of years. Now, because of us . . ."

"It's a sad story," he said.

"I hope it isn't. We can still reverse things."

She looked out the frosted glass.

"I'd like to follow them one day, go on that journey to Tierra del Fuego . . . You know, for research."

The square was deserted, save for a homeless man. A heap of

thick, coarse blankets that from here looked purple, mauve, not gray. She changed the subject:

"He's always there, that man out there. Even when it snows," she said. "His name is Theo."

Hadi asked, "How do you know that?"

"I asked him."

They talked while the songs played. The album looped. In the lulls, they shared an easy quiet. The third time around, he asked about her home in Damascus.

"Well, it's a yellow house."

A pale, custardy yellow that covered the building's facade. The interior was powder blue, "like some apartments in Paris." He said he had never been. "Me neither," she laughed, "but I will."

She described three arched windows that looked onto the balcony on which her parents had their coffee every morning. Her mama boiled it twice, like the Turks do, until a sliver of foam formed on its surface. Meanwhile, her baba shaved and listened to Fairuz on his transistor radio. She told him how they then sat, every day, he on the left, she on the right. Coffee, his cigarette, the *rakweh* on the floor between them. Its heat had discolored only that tile over the years.

She asked about his home, but he said, "Another night." He didn't want to leave hers yet, warmer, sunnier. His home was cold and drafty, dark because the windows were covered with cardboard and newspapers. The *shabiha* had smashed the glass and blasted the door open his last night in that house.

He had known they were coming—they already had for Ghaith, and Omar had disappeared—but not when. If he had . . . that last night smelled of beans and rice; the toppled pot of fasoulia. The floor and walls were splattered bloodred with trickling tomato sauce.

What an idiot he had been. And what for? *What for?* Mama had gasped and muted her wails with her hands. He had promised her *No more*, after Far' Falastin. *Khalas, Hadi!* He would stay home and mind his own business and help Baba with the harvest. And he had, but then, last week, carrying four crates of apples to the back of Abu Yussef's store, he had seen the napalm, the petrol, the wicks, the glass bottles . . .

There had been no time to apologize to her. The first bombs had begun to rain, and they all ran to the shelter. The following morning, all were too raw and hoarse to speak, and that night, the *shabiha* had come and Mama had lied.

She had lied, and they had slapped her while he crouched under the sink in a kitchen cabinet, arms wrapped around his knees. Those had shaken so hard that once or twice they knocked the pine cupboard doors. He had frozen, but with so much shouting on the other side, no one had heard.

He had heard every word. His mother, a *sharmouta! Ahbeh! Khiryeh!* His woolen collar stuffed in his mouth, eyes shut, his toe touching a bottle of rubbing alcohol. Sometimes he thinks he should have drunk it.

"What are your parents like?"

They had smashed his baba's glasses and knocked away his cane, so the old man had stood, frozen, in a fog pierced by his wife's screams, swearing to Allah—her shrieks reaching the sky—that her son was not there.

The men had beat her and left. And Hadi had crouched. Through it all, Hadi had crouched.

Never again.

He had fallen out of the cupboard, onto the tiles, sprawled, legs jelly. Baba had pulled him up.

Hadi still didn't know how he did it. Kays Deeb had stood his son up. That same night, Hadi Deeb had walked lead-footed out of that house.

"Tell me about Syria then. What's it like now? Really? My parents never tell me much, and I've been gone so long."

But he didn't want to answer that either. He already knew, from the too-limpid, too-wide eyes looking at him, that he shouldn't.

Sama reminisced:

"There used to be an ice-cream cart on the corner of our street. Abu Fuad Khooja made the creamiest ashta . . ."

He couldn't. He couldn't tell her Damascus, now, was broken and cold, covered with dust and caking pools of blood. He couldn't let her see the city, naked and battered, with its barren store shelves, barren faces queuing for bread, for water, for gas. Its gassings, gas masks. Checkpoints, on corners where the ice-cream carts used to be. Piles of blue, pink, white trash bags, willfully ignored by all but the most desperately starved, and the cats. The feral cats who clawed them open and left trails of rotting bones.

That was what it was like, Damascus. He couldn't let her see it. She was waiting for an answer. He looked out instead. The strip of sky he could see was starless, but the blue was deep. Not navy, but slightly jewel-toned. It seemed to move, expand as he had never seen it do in Syria. Yet it was the same sky.

"Do you miss it?" she asked, bringing him back, trying to understand his silence.

He looked at her.

"Do you?"

Neither answered.

They did not notice the music stop. They did not look away from each other until they heard the poor college boy stacking chairs and stools around them. Taking their cue, they layered up. Not enough. At the door, they were momentarily slapped in place by a gust of cold.

She let out a squeak and huddled into him. Apples and vanilla again. They scurried across the square to the station, past her homeless friend, snoring gloriously. Down the escalator. She bought him his first CharlieTicket. It lives today in a drawer, book, pocket somewhere in Boston.

Four days later, Hadi returned to Harvard Square, retracing the journey he and Mr. Jeffries had made by car to the gala fundraiser. He walked, and it was a different journey, or perhaps he was a different person. The directions he had carefully written down felt like a treasure map, rustling solemnly, thrillingly in his gloves.

Cambridge, Massachusetts, was still a land riddled with strangeness, one that turned hostile at dusk, when it was cloaked in a certain, particularly mean shade of blue. That alien color all immigrants know, a thick, shocking blue that outlined and isolated every object, amplifying one's sense of separateness. It haunted Hadi, and would for years, probably forever. But that had been in the evening, and now it was ten in the morning.

It was past eleven, and the sky was enchantingly sky blue, the jet lag had passed, and he was on his first solo expedition and felt brave and daring.

Now, the strangeness was delicious, intoxicating. He had a borrowed phone, a borrowed coat, twenty dollars, and a map. In spite of it, he got lost. Blessedly, wonderfully, amid the new, exotic trees, smells, faces, shop fronts.

Used books and used clothes and records and graffiti and weed as he walked on Main Street. Chinese takeout, Indian spices. Starbucks, Chipotle. A caricature of a Middle Eastern restaurant, tattoo parlors, the pizza shop with its red and yellow and the same poor kid at the counter. A local movie theater. Coffee shops, coffee shops, coffee shops. Accents and skin and hair colors and eye shapes and . . . he stopped.

A stooped woman wheeling a black cloth cart of groceries, out of which peeked oranges, a roll of toilet paper, and milk. The strangest sight of all, the most flabbergasting. People lived here. The woman reached a blue door in a brick building, burrowed in her pocket for keys, and the boy inside Hadi thought, *There is no suffering here.*

He walked even slower now, more astonished. He crossed campus, where these students were not characters in a play. They walked, carrying textbooks and bags, which were heavy, which were not stage props, carrying coffees he could smell, carrying on with conversations. They could have been students on campus at the University of Damascus.

But no. Words and sentence fragments drifted around him. English, but also, the melody; there was no tension. He became acutely aware of tone; no one was shouting. Another sudden, jarring realization: No one was afraid. They were just walking, these students, on a campus in a parallel universe.

In a white square, he saw them queue in front of a Vietnamese food truck. He watched, amazed, as one ordered, in English, a sandwich. He had never tasted Vietnamese food. He witnessed, minutes later, a sandwich materialize, very real and very big, and smelling of beef, a strange sauce, and, strongly, vinegar. The boy took a giant, distracted bite and hurried on. Hadi stood, shell-shocked by the sublime banality of this world, while in another, at this very moment . . . but he was not in that other. He was here, and dizzy with so much stimulation, and, suddenly, ravenous.

And suddenly, he saw himself stand in that line, heard himself order in English, saw his hand present his twenty-dollar bill and receive his sandwich. He saw himself, in America, taking a bite from a Vietnamese sandwich, a puffy baguette—then he thought of bread lines and just as suddenly, felt nauseated.

Ten minutes late, but she would forgive him. Sama Zayat remembered being new in a new land. She stood outside the library, gulping precious, rare November sun. She had thought it would be easier for them to meet in front of the building where they'd first met, that night he had given his speech at the fundraiser for refugees.

He appeared, panting and raggedly apologetic. "I'm—" He coughed and wheezed, attempting to continue in sign language.

She burst into laughter and said, "There should be a water fountain inside the library. Do you need a drink before we go to the museum?"

While Hadi searched for the restroom, Sama walked around the empty hall where, four days ago, there had been such a crowd. Her footsteps echoed now, and the collections of rare books and manuscripts lining the walls glowed in royal blue, black, forest green, burgundy. Hundreds of thousands of records of human culture and history, overwhelming.

She stopped at a gospel lectionary enclosed in a glass case. At first, she had thought the writing was in Arabic. It was in Syriac, dating back to the eleventh century. According to the plaque, the book had been used to celebrate Mass in an Orthodox church somewhere in today's southern Turkey or northwestern Syria.

The book was open and petrified at a specific page, marked by a once-red, deeply frayed satin ribbon. The text displayed would have been the last one read by the congregation. The manuscript was highly damaged, disfigured by a gaping hole in its middle. A bullet had run it through, and around the exit wound, bits of parchment flayed out like rose petals. Sama turned to the plaque. Eighteen ninety-five. The Hamidian massacres. Hundreds of thousands killed, a million pillaged, fifty thousand exiled . . . where?

Hadi, emerging, his voice echoing down the hall:

"I'm so sorry I kept you waiting! This place is enormous!"

She jumped and gave him perhaps too big a smile.

"Ready to see something lovely?"

She practically flew out into the sun, dragging him behind her.

* * *

Glassy blue through glass ceiling, three stories high. Into the atrium, sun flowed in white streams. White marble arches. The balconies, normally swarmed with visitors, were quiet. A campus secret, one of the better kept: the art museum on a Wednesday morning.

Klimt, Degas, Van Gogh, Whistler, Monet—she had them, gloriously, all to herself. She held his hand and did not seem to notice how it turned both of them red, pulling him in and out of rooms and up and down stairs. Stopping abruptly at a single drop of white on a pearl earring, a shadow of an indentation on a marble nape, a forest so lush and dense they could have stepped into it, a million colors in an orchard of pear trees.

They finally stopped, and she stopped for breath, in front of Sintenis's *Daphne*. Sama had saved her for last. The sculpture stood in the center of a glass room on the ground floor. Young; naked; sprouting bronze leaves from the tips of fingers thin as filaments, reaching skyward; swirling strands of hair, upswept by an invisible gale; luminous in her metamorphosis. Behind the glass walls that framed her, trees ablaze with autumn.

"Why is she turning into a tree?" Hadi asked.

Sama said, "Daphne is a nymph, and she is trying to escape the god Apollo. He has fallen desperately in love with her and vowed to make her his. Her only way out is to beg her father, the river god, to turn her into a tree."

"So she's dying?"

"Her human form is. She becomes something else."

He frowned at the adolescent figure lurching up, desperate, her body fragile and taut.

"That's morbid."

"I don't think so."

"What? Sama, she dies!"

Sama shook her head.

"She's free. I think she's beautiful."

Beyond the glass, a brown bird alighted on a bare branch.

"That bird looks like a *douri*," he said, looking, not at Sama. She took a step toward him and they both looked out the glass. Sama flushed.

"*Douri* . . . How embarrassing, I never learned the names in Arabic. Is that the one that sings?"

"No, that's *hassoun*, with a red dot over its beak. *Douri* is the little one everyone hunts. So stupid. It's inedible. The bird is so small, it's just feather and bones, almost no meat."

"That's horrible! There should be a law—"

"There is," he said. "Since the war started, they've been shooting *hassoun* too . . . At least that one they can eat."

They had hot chocolate in the atrium. Hadi hesitated, but Sama had already ordered two, which appeared, thick and mounted with two obscenely large dollops of cream, in wide and deep porcelain bowls. On each saucer, there was a cookie. She wanted to clap, and did, and it was his turn to laugh. He also applauded.

They sat at a flimsy table under the glass ceiling, two Syrians far away from Syria, having bitter chocolate and cream, in an empty museum they could pretend was theirs. They could see the sky through the roof. In that enormous moment, they could, perhaps, see the world, not as it was, but as it could be. Different. Wonderfully pigmented with possibility, like the paintings, the spectra of light and color surrounding them. Upper lip mustached, tongue coated with cocoa, she asked which was his favorite.

"The pear trees, definitely. They remind me of my father's orchard."

He paused, and through the chink, she glimpsed that home of his she didn't know, and waited. He wiped foam off his lip and put it back there with another sip.

"I think I'd like to bring my parents here, someday. I don't think they've ever been to an art museum."

He looked down and lightly prodded the cookie, which was wrapped. He almost opened it, then seemed to change his mind and put it carefully in his coat pocket. Then he lifted his cup, but it was empty. He put it back down, traced the rim, then laid his hand on the table.

If she had known him better, she would have reached for it. If she had known him better, she would have told him he could be happy here. He could be anything, have anything he wanted. Could he see it? His life in this vast country? He wouldn't have to be afraid.

"I think your parents will like Boston. There are parks and libraries, and all the museums, and for your father, the nature . . ." And she was rambling like a tour guide, dancing around the word *war*, desperate for him to look up, return from wherever he had gone. She realized it and stopped, and silence fell between them. He did look up, then.

He looked around and saw, with searing double vision, the atrium, light streaming down in curtains, this world, their old one, and sky piercing blue over the glass.

"Look at where we are," he said.

"I'm going to bring my parents here," he said now.

They rose and began buttoning their coats. She wrapped a long red scarf made of thick looped wool around her neck.

"What about your parents?"

She tied and untied the scarf and tied it again. When, after the third time, she looked up, she wore an expression he didn't understand. It looked like sadness, but deeper, laced almost with anger.

"They won't come. Baba won't . . . He has thoughts about land and duty . . ." She struggled, letting the thought fall, grasping for it like a drifting thread. "Some people."

She undid her scarf and let it hang angrily.

"*We* weren't born with roots, *el a'ama*! We're not trees!"

That was all. The wind fell as it had risen. She took his hand again and led them out of the glass doors, and heat seeped between them where their gloves touched.

March 2016

He fell off the bed, dragging the sheets along. Again. She gasped, then laughed. He found nothing amusing about the situation.

"That's it. I'm staying on the floor."

"No, come back!"

And she tried to pull him up, onto the Crusoe-esque raft of a mattress. His weight brought them both tumbling down, into a heap of lilac and duvet, and on his hairy chest she was light and shaking with silent giggles. And naked. He tried to cover her, which only tangled the sheets more. Soon they were bound like silkworms on the floor, only his left foot free, and he knocked that against the iron bedframe.

Again.

"*Yil'aan abouk!*"

Muffled, bubbling laughs.

"It's not funny! Sama, your bed wouldn't fit a child!"

"I'm sorry, but the room is too small for a larger bed!" came the protest through a tunnel she finally dug between the sheet and chest of the man who, she now knew, smelled of green orange and mint cologne, with a hint of oak, and was now puffed with indignation, damp, and tickly on her cheek. She had the urge to laugh and sneeze all at once, and the sense that she should do neither, and—

Too late.

They clambered back onto the bed, finally, and she slipped into his white pullover and kept her fists in the sleeves.

"Your room is a joke as well! I've seen closets that are bigger!"

It was a closet, one in which, between the bed and piles of books she insisted she needed right where they were, all of them, right by her—a book of haiku; Camus's *Notebooks, 1935–1942*; a collection of Rilke poems—there was barely space for a person to stand.

The entire apartment was minuscule. It had just one other room that served as a living/dining space, a blue-and-white bathroom, and—its only redeeming quality, in his opinion—a terrace.

More of a ledge. A strip of balcony on which two wooden stools miraculously fit. On which, when the weather warmed, she said, it was divine to sit, sipping coffee. She had managed to find, yes, in Boston, a *rakweh*, and would make them real Turkish coffee. With cardamom, that was how she liked it. His would have to be sweet, she knew that now. She loved that she knew that now. They had had to purchase sugar when they bought a toothbrush, razor, and shaving cream for him to keep in the cabinet behind the bathroom mirror. And a pot and a pan, for she didn't own any. He had been appalled, but she had said simply, "I don't like to eat alone."

Hadi did, grudgingly, acknowledge that the skylights were a nice

touch. The sparsity of man-made light in the residential neighborhood meant they could see the stars.

"I can see the universe from my bed," she had said.

"I like my room," she said now, small and defiant and digging her
feet under his thighs for warmth.

"It's too small for me to feel alone, and the bed warms up fast,"
said the girl who, for a different life, had crossed an ocean. And
forgot to look both ways before crossing the road, slept curled in
a ball, breathing softly into him, smelled of lemon and red apples
and vanilla, lived on a cloud and, when he wasn't there, on crackers
with salt.

"If you want me, you have to take the bed too."

He watched her scowl at him, rebellious, putting on his socks,
the freest girl he had ever met, pulling them up to her knees, Sama
Zayat . . .

He said, "Marry me."

She did not make a sound or look up from the socks. He wondered if she had heard him. He had known her four months, known
he loved her just as long. He knew he was mad to ask. He knew
who he was—a refugee—and what and where he had come from—
a farmer's home in Douma, Syria. He lived firmly on the ground
and, only recently, on minimum wage and tips. And he knew he
didn't care. He knew what he wanted, and it was on this raft under
a skylight in the universe.

"Sama?"

"What did you say?"

"Marry me, please. We can keep the bed . . ."

Five months later, he didn't need to turn around as he heard the bathroom door open, the feet stop at the threshold. He didn't need to see her fingers hold the test. He knew they were trembling. So were his.

They would be mad not to be scared, but he knew, as certainly as he knew gravity, as birds defy it when they take off in flocks of hundreds, thousands of copper-feathered wings no longer than those shaking fingers, that he was happy.

He turned, and she was still wearing his shirt she had borrowed that morning, and now, pregnant, crying, and smiling.

She said: "We're going to need a bigger apartment."

They would tell the world later. There would be time for that. Just then, they told the bronze statues of ducklings in Boston Public Garden. They told the willows and swan boats and followed the crowd of late-evening saunterers. Joggers passed them. They passed tourists. In their minds they told them. And the couples holding hands, and those pushing strollers, and those sharing ice cream on benches with toddlers. They moved among and with the colorful, seamless patchwork of humans.

Up and down the park's sinewy paths. They floated past the smell of rice and curry in large aluminum pans, doled out in heaps to a large Indian family. Nearby: catch, fetch, Frisbees whizzing through the air. Farther along: pepperoni and beer. Laughing twenty-somethings.

And bathing all of it, evening sun. And amid it all, them. He kissed her. She tasted sweet, of cherry, and afterward, the air he breathed in did. They wandered, turning random corners, till they reached the other end of the garden. They paused at the gate.

They could walk down Newbury Street, or take Boylston to Copley Square, or: The trees on Commonwealth Avenue were ablaze with sunset in variegated shades of orange, amber, and gold. They turned there. They walked until the trees turned deep violet, then navy, and against them the night sky seemed a light cobalt. Only then, finally, did their feet touch the ground, and they became aware of their soles burning and the riot in their stomachs. They entered the very next restaurant.

A diner. They commandeered a booth by the window, and each collapsed on a red faux-leather bench. She ordered scrambled eggs.

"For dinner?" he asked, surprised.

"Hey, it's a free country," the waitress said, tucking the menu she had been about to give Sama under her arm. Hadi accepted the other.

"Yes, for dinner! I'm going to have breakfast every chance I get before morning sickness hits."

"Scrambled eggs, then," said the waitress, scribbling, and Sama gave Hadi the smile she must have worn when she ran away from school as a child, triumphant. To this, with utmost solemnity, he responded by ordering pancakes with chocolate syrup.

She offered him her first bite; he saved his last for her. It happened without thought, as a matter of course. After the eggs had been devoured, and the toast, she slid under the table and re-emerged next to him. Around them, the air smelled of french fries; his breath, of chocolate syrup. Her head then rested on his shoulder and they lingered, lulled by the meal. People flowed by on the street, hazy dabs of watercolor, like fleeting landscapes from a train. In the streetlight, it all looked ambery. Then she said, continuing a thought no one in the world could hear:

"Are you really happy?"

He could not see her face.

"Are you really asking?"

He felt a slight brush of air as her head lifted from his shoulder. He turned and saw the quiet, fluttering search for land to light on.

"I am the happiest man alive."

Her chin crumpled, barely.

". . . and I'm afraid."

"Me too," she whispered, and when he asked what of, she didn't answer for a while, and he thought she wouldn't.

"Everything," she said.

"All of it. Life. Having a child, raising a child. Money. Where will we live? How? My research stipend, your tips? This baby—"

"Will have everything we came to America for."

Everything. Every opportunity, and the right to it, with dignity.

"The parks and schools, the museums and libraries . . . remember, Sama?"

Slowly she nodded, and her clenched fingers uncurled on his thigh.

"I'll tell you what I'm scared of," he said, looking at her hand. "I'm scared our child will have such a different life here that I won't have a place in it. I've never thrown a baseball . . ."

"You'll learn. We both will."

"I've never built a snowman."

She smiled. "Winter will come. Believe me, you'll have mounds of snow and months to practice."

But he was looking away. His fork meandered along the chocolaty remains on his uncleared plate, leaving a white trail. In the silence, out the window, they each imagined their own winter on that dwindling August day.

She said, "I'm scared of raising a child alone here."

He said, "I'm scared our child will be ashamed of me"—unsteady pause—"their father the refugee. The foreigner—"

She put her mouth to his.

October 2016

She should have brought a coat. Too late. They couldn't turn back now; home was too far behind, and they could not risk being late.

That pivotal October day when autumn turns into truth. Only birds can feel it coming. Birds, and some humans, and even then, barely; a faint trepidation of the heart. Such a day does not come announced. No trumpets sound. One morning, it just is. The wind rises.

The feeling in her chest rose too, intense and deep and expansive, reverberated, beat in her chest like wings. She really should have brought a coat.

She huddled into him and tried to pick up their pace, but he was happy sauntering, looking up at the foliage. That word did not even exist in Arabic. Nor did such reds and oranges, in any autumn he had ever known. Here, the trees reflected all along the Charles River and seemed to set it on fire.

The walk was mercifully short. They pushed through the revolving doors and the air went from moist to dry, the smell from leaves and soil to a blue antiseptic. Up the escalators, an elevator, down a glass corridor from which they could see, beyond the burgundy of Beacon Hill, the fiery hues of the Common.

It was warm enough in the waiting room—a brief reprieve—

but they were not there long, for once. The exam room walls were painted an icy blue. He rubbed her shoulders; she rubbed her legs. Her feet dangled like a schoolgirl's from the examination table.

"Hello, hello!" came an exceedingly festive voice. "How far along are we?"

The voice was matched with a broad, jovial face, quite round, topped with happily-middle-aging once-blond hair.

"Around nine weeks. We're not sure," Sama answered nervously.

"Well, let's find out!"

Latex. *Snap*. Something blue, gelatinous. Sama gasped and tried to think of—

"Ah, there we go."

Then they heard it, the drumroll.

Not an actual drum. A toy drum, perhaps. Lighter. Faster. A hummingbird's wings. Eighty beats per minute. One hundred. One hundred and thirty-five. The baby's heart, in a trilling crescendo. Her heart joined.

That night, they rode the screechy Green Line train to Symphony Hall, where Hadi attended his first classical concert. Béla Bartók, Concerto No. 2. His fingers accompanied the violins on an invisible piano. The bows flitted on the strings, hummingbird wings, hummingbird heart, beating. One hundred thirty-five beats per minute. Takeoff. Land disappears.

Much as it has been studied, the phenomenon of bird migration remains, in many of its aspects, a mystery to scientists. At its heart, the very question of why some birds go at all.

Not all birds migrate, only some, few; less than 1,800 of the world's 10,000 species. Less than one in five birds. The rest, for millennia, have stayed where they are.

It has been assumed that those who go must, in order to survive. Indeed, patterns have been observed of movement from east to west, for food; north to south, and back, for warmth and shelter. There are, however, baffling exceptions.

Some birds fly north, to lands that have been frozen solid for months. Some, instead of flying at night to avoid predators, go in broad daylight.

Some birds travel in song; the mavis flies with a repertoire of more than one hundred tunes.

The Arctic tern flies across the globe but takes the scenic route, 20,000 kilometers longer than it should. The ancient murrelet flies over the North Pacific, 16,000 kilometers, for no observable reason.

January 29, 2017

HADI

It's fucking freezing in here. I shake and suffocate and tell myself it's the fucking AC. Fucking Americans and their fucking AC. You were right, Sama, I did pick up the language quick.

They're sending me back, Samati. They're deporting me. The flight boards in less than an hour. I signed the form. Don't hate me.

I didn't have a choice. Whatever they tell you, if they tell you, whatever you hear, from anyone, know this: I didn't have a choice. I didn't choose to leave. I shouted and demanded, then I begged, for a lawyer, a phone call, a fucking paper to write you a note. They gave me the form.

I signed it. I don't know what was on it. They wouldn't let me read it. They wouldn't let me call a lawyer. They uncuffed me, gave me a pen, pointed to the line. I signed. They took the form, replaced the cuffs. An officer stamped CANCELED – BOS in bright red on my travel permit. The sickeningly mundane thud, then nothing. They took everything. I cried.

I asked for my passport, could I at least have my passport back.

65

They said I'd get it on the plane. Then they gave me a sandwich. A soggy cheese sandwich. Sama, I ate it.

I ate it. I was starved. And I asked for another, which they gave me with such a smile. They're going to joke about me for days. They'll call me the Cheese Man. The one who cried when they took his life away, so they gave him a sandwich.

The door.

"It's time to go, buddy. These boys will escort you. You can make that phone call now."

No, I can't. If I do, if I call you, hear your voice, sleepy on the pillows, our pillows, I know I won't be able to go. They'll have to drag me on board.

"I don't want it anymore."

"You sure? Nothing you want to tell the Mrs.?"

What could I possibly say? *I hope you got home safe, Samati. I hope you ate. Dinner, or breakfast. I don't know what time it is. Please take care of yourself. Take care of our little one. I didn't have a choice. I'm sorry . . .*

I shake my head at the officer, who shrugs.

I am the last to board, to be boarded, handcuffed, escorted by two officers, like I could actually run. We cross the whole, fully boarded plane. I don't look up. I wanted to. I wanted to show them I was not afraid, not wrong, not a criminal, not scared, but a woman in the fifth row put her arm on her daughter's chest like a seat belt when I passed.

Last row, before the toilets, which have already begun to smell. A seat by the last window. My heart leaps. They took everything, but, Sama, they gave me the window.

One officer uncuffs me. The other hands my passport to the flight attendant. The young woman politely, shakily, asks me to fasten my seat belt. And to please leave the shade up for takeoff. I want to smile, but she will not meet my eyes and disappears. I think of all the mice, ants, and beetles crushed by terrified girls like her. I shouldn't have looked up. The passenger across the aisle asks for another seat.

I can't see Boston. Perhaps I'm glad. Perhaps I couldn't bear it. I can see the sky, workers on the tarmac, lugging suitcases off a cart under the white and orange lights.

I cannot see the stars. The runway lights are too bright. The irony, that they should make the night less visible. It lies ahead, above, around me. The plane shifts its weight painfully. Slow, like it's scared to move. Suddenly, it jerks forward. Careens down the runway, tearing through the air. The pull sucks me into my seat, knocks the air out of me. Blood pounds through my heart. Rush. Takeoff.

Tons upon tons of aluminum, steel, jet fuel, human bodies, suddenly weightless. Most of the passengers probably didn't look up. On my first flight, few did. The children, one or two adults, but all the refugees. They looked out and down at the disappearing lights and sobbed and kept touching the glass as though to be sure it was real, then putting their fingers to their lips.

I can see Boston now. I watch it shrink, you in it, shimmer briefly, disappear. How easily, too easily. It's gone. It could never have been.

I could have never come to America. I could have landed anywhere. You could have been wearing a different dress the night we met. Strangers seated in orderly rows, seat belts fastened, tray tables stowed. There are infinitely many lives. In this plane, in the sky, for the next few hours at least, all are the same.

A red light blinks on the wing. When we land, some of us will be home. They will not smell of plane long. To the rest, it will cling, like the dankness on unclaimed luggage.

I hope our child never knows this smell, Sama, that who we are does not cling to him. I hope he never feels this fear. I hope he speaks with no accent, that when he learns to say words like *immigrant*, *border*, his *r*s don't roll, just slide off his tongue, lightly.

SAMA

These are not our sheets. Ours smell of softener and Sundays. These sheets are starched. This is not the right Sunday.

I feel no heat, no chest hair, no heartbeat. My other cheek feels cold. The chill sneaks under the covers. These are not our covers. I should just keep my eyes shut. Some light filters through. I should just keep my mind on last Sunday.

Last Sunday, light flitted up and down the ridges of the covers, up your neck, onto your face. I tapped on the birthmarks, inventing constellations. You wouldn't wake up, so I played the piano on your cheek. Then I kissed your nose, then I just brushed the ridge underneath and you sneezed and were furious and I really was sorry, but Hadi, I was so hungry.

My stomach hurts. Last Sunday, I wished aloud for croissants. I promised coffee, the thickest, sweetest coffee you had ever tasted. I mentioned the baby, shamelessly. I kissed and cajoled till you knocked the covers off and stood just to be away from me.

The bed always turns cold the instant you leave. This bed is cold. It's not ours, and you're not here.

Last Sunday unravels. It frays and splays in my mind. Your mother called while you were at the bakery. Everything went cold then. The coffee, the promised croissants, left to harden in the bag, on the floor by the door where you dropped them, still there hours later, when you left. I can't catch the thoughts. They run from me in every direction. Light strains through my eyelashes. This is not our bed. I should just turn on my stomach and un-wake. My stomach hurts. Why does my . . .

"Ms. Zayat, please stop screaming! Calm down!"

My limbs disobey, thrash, knocking against the nurse, the plastic railing on the bed. Contact sends me screaming louder. Electricity shoots up and down my body, peaking in the soft, horrifying sac of skin where—

"Where is my son?!"

"I have your painkillers! Hold still so I can work your IV!"

But I cannot. My eyes are wide open now, and the bed, the room, my body are devastatingly empty.

"Where is my baby?!"

"Ms. Zayat, please keep still. The doctors are on their way."

I sob. I scream. I fight the nurse and her needle. Liquid fire through the IV. Heat, pain sears my lacerated uterus, my manic heart, my brain, fighting to absorb shock after shock.

"Where is my husband? Has he called? My baby!"

A door bursting open. Cold air rushes in from the corridor. A man's voice:

"Ms. Zayat!"

I know that voice. Yesterday floods the room. Every second of yesterday fills every crevice. I drown. Thoughts and limbs flail. A hand grabs my shoulder. Another locks me in position.

"Ms. Zayat. I need you to breathe. Again! Through the nose, out the mouth."

I cough and sputter. My nose is blocked, my lungs overflowing, but the voice and grip urge me on, relentless. The spasms subside.

Slowly, the hands withdraw. The room clears. There is no bassinet.

"My son."

The words come out a rasp.

"He's all right, Ms. Zayat."

Another voice. Another woman. She steps out of a row of white coats and a uniform look of sympathy. Her hair is dyed an aggressive blond and her features are hard, but the eyes and voice are soft.

"I'm Dr. Farber, chief of neonatology. This is Dr. Scott. He and his team delivered your son."

Tall, pale, shiny blond hair streaked with reddish lowlights. He must be my age.

"How are you feeling, Ms. Zayat?"

"Please, where is my baby? Please, why isn't he here? And my husband—"

"Someone is trying to reach him," Dr. Farber interjects, "and your baby is in the neonatal intensive care unit."

She can only be a few years older than me, but the cut of her jaw is so severe she looks older. The bags under her eyes cast shadows down her cheeks. Her lipstick, too, is tired and cracked.

"Ms. Zayat, as you know, you went into labor early. Quite early: twenty-eight weeks. That's about three months too soon. Babies born at that stage do not have good chances of survival."

The room floods with ice water.

"You said—"

"Yes, I did."

She forces calm on us both.

"Your baby is in the NICU. We were able to stabilize him and transfer him to an incubator. Our priorities are breathing—"

"He can't breathe?!"

"He's on a respirator. His lungs are still too underdeveloped to work on their own."

Underdeveloped. Too small. A mask on a face, too small. My own lungs swell and burn.

"The machine takes some of the strain off. We're also giving him doses of surfactant. That's so the lungs don't collapse."

Collapse, like my heart into talcum and cinder as she goes through her list of hemoglobin levels, electrolytes, glucose, two units of blood on standby, "inserted a catheter into his stomach."

My heart and I dissolve into convulsive sobs. Everyone else is silent.

"Is he in pain?"

I have to know.

"We are doing all we can."

"What does that mean?! I want to see him!"

"It would be better to wait . . ."

I can't wait, I can't breathe. What happened to the air?

HADI

A liminal sky, neither night nor day. In it, somewhere over no land, the plane moves in a blue and silence so crystalline it seems still.

After takeoff, I begged the flight attendant to return my passport. She refused, her instructions clear: not until touchdown. She doesn't understand. She doesn't have to. Her life is not defined by words on a document, it does not hang on a stamp or visa.

She can go wherever she wants. I want to be angry at her. Outraged, at every American: the one who questioned me, those who told him to, those who put me on a plane, those on this plane with me. For being, just by being, proof of what I am *not*.

It isn't their fault.

They didn't make the rules. They drew lots by being born. So did I. I shift my fury elsewhere. To my own country. My passport.

I denounce this myth of a state, a nation that dared call itself my home. That filled my head, growing up, with delusions of freedom and roots. My father. *You filled my head, Baba! You taught me to love your land! Your four plum trees and an apple tree, roots digging deeper and deeper into the dust, searching for water. There was no fucking water! There is no freedom. These roots are snares, and this land, this fucking land—look at what your land did!*

But Baba can't hear me. Baba is dead. He died in a motel room, in another country, one single motherfucking day before his visa interview. Precious visa. Precious freedom. One day after he finally crossed the border. Precious fucking Syrian passport.

I hate my passport.

I need my passport. I'm nobody without it. *No! Don't mistake the fucking dust for water!* I'm nobody without that travel permit. Trapped without it, because of it. I'm nothing without that stamp. Nowhere. I lean my head against the cool window. It is night. We fly over Lebanon, or Cyprus.

Ridges cast deep shadows, mountains. Lebanon then. Splatters of twinkling lights. Tripoli? Beirut? Saida? All flights over Syria have been rerouted. I'm glad; I'm not ready to see Damascus.

"We have begun our descent into Amman. Please close your tray tables, adjust your seats, and fasten your seat belts."

My heart lurches as we tip into deep, dark ink. We sink toward arrival like into the sea at night. My heart, the plane. Land. Exile. The flight attendant, looking relieved, returns my passport.

SAMA

The elevator halts, crushingly, at every floor from the fifteenth to the NICU on the tenth. A bored metallic voice keeps track, announcing each like a station on a train ride. People board, disembark. Trapped in a wheelchair, I keep my eyes on the screen so my life does not brush theirs. The numbers slide off, like the countdown to a black-and-white movie.

This whole box is drained of color, like the room I just left. Empty. No balloons, off-white and sky blue; no chocolates in silver paper. No baklava on a silver tray for visitors. No visitors, flowers, baby. No heat. White light through a gaping black frame.

I couldn't leave it fast enough, that mutilation of a new mother's room. I wanted to walk. I wanted to run, fly to the tenth floor. But I could hardly stand. A faceless nurse holds the wheelchair in place, blankets weigh my thighs down, but my knees still knock against each other.

The thud of arrival.

Steel doors open to the floor where the NICU lives. I grip my stomach. It doesn't help. The nurse wheels me out. Nobody follows. The other passengers are going elsewhere. The doors close.

I am wheeled down a silent hallway, too slow, too fast, too cold. We stop at Room 1013. At the threshold, I lose courage.

"Stop!"

I cry, to her surprise, to my horror and shame; I am scared of entering.

Too much of a coward to meet her eyes, I look down. The wheels graze against the navy tiles between the hallway and room. I could touch the fear. If I cross that border, if I see the boy inside and he becomes real—

"Ms. Zayat, your son is waiting for you."

He already is. My heart knows that heart. *My* son is waiting, for me. The threshold dissolves. From inside Room 1013, a force powerful and light as air. From inside me, a pull I have never felt. I nod to the nurse, and we roll in.

No clock, no windows. An incubator sits in the center of a too-large, too-empty room. Monitors blink like Christmas lights, red and green and blue.

The nurse wheels me as close to the box as the wires and tubes allow. Too many between us, and a plastic barrier. I feel, gapingly, unarrived. Almost there. The ache is so great I could sob. I lean forward.

My entire life feels stopped at that clear wall, those last few inches of distance enormous, agonizing, but then, a tremor. But then, but then, behind it all, almost fully concealed by the respirator . . .

"This is Baby Deeb."

An all-purpose blanket, white and blue. Under the mask, a tube, neon orange, thin as a hair, slips into his nose. A piece of tape holds it in place. It is shorter than my thumb. It is larger than his cheek. He is smaller than my forearm.

I have never been more acutely aware of life. It is almost palpable, white and blue and beautiful. It travels through the wall, coloring the air, disarming me. All my life suddenly feels like a series of almost arrivals, and now, and this, and here, is as close as I will ever get to happiness.

"Hello, *habibi*."

Baby Deeb. Hadi, he already has your name. Part of a name. Part you, part me. I look, opening my eyes wide, a skyful. His are closed. He has long lashes, thin as the strands of a feather. The finest nose I have seen. His lower lip flutters, barely. I reach over. Instinct, a flapping of heart, of wings. My hand meets the plastic.

"Hello, *habibi*, I'm here."

Hoping he can hear me, hoping, against all reason, he can feel some of my heat.

"Mama's here, *ya zghir*."

I'm here.

"Would you like to touch your baby?"

I do not dare understand the question. I do not dare turn around to look at the nurse.

"Ms. Zayat, did you hear me?"

"Are, are you sure it's safe?"

Not daring to hope.

"I don't see why not. You could just slide your hand through the porthole. In fact, I think contact with his mother will be good for him."

His mother. The words glow, fine and numinous as fireflies in my lungs.

"Sterilize your hands with that gel over there. Clean them well. Put on some gloves."

I hurry, before she changes her mind, my fingers so shaky I tear two latex gloves before I succeed. She opens the porthole.

"Go ahead," she whispers, as though not wishing to let anything louder into the incubator. I hesitate, then jaggedly, clumsily, guide my arm into the hole, into my baby's bell jar. My finger touches his.

Heartbeats course through me and out, in waves, like a meteor shower, breaking through the latex barrier between us. *Hey, it's me. It's Mama.* I think the words as lightly as I can, not wanting to mar his skin, translucent as rice paper. So little, so very *zghir.* So soft I hardly feel his fine, fine fingers stir. Like touching wind.

I withdraw my arm, exhausted by the infinitely small gesture, the infinitely colossal encounter. Something lingers on my fingers, light. The nurse closes the porthole.

"Your son is beautiful."

I can only nod. My throat is raw, my vision blurred, like I have been staring at the sun. I see her through particles of floating pink and green.

"He'll be okay. You just have to be patient."

I can be patient. I have time. A lifetime. *I'll wait here,* ya zghir, *on the other side of the incubator, until you're ready. Then we'll go together. You'll see, the world is also waiting.*

"Have you decided on a name?"

August 2016

Listen to this!"

She bolted upright, a blade of grass caught in her messy bun, which had lightened to burnt umber. He felt a mild breeze; she was waving the book over his face. Lethargically, he slid an eye open.

It was all she needed. She plopped the book on his chest. How could she be so energetic after such a lunch? How could she read in this heat? It seemed to fall on them in buckets. Her cheeks were so sunburned they looked like freckled peaches. She wore big Holly Golightly shades, but even through the amber-tinted glasses he could see her eyes dancing. He shielded his with the back of his hand.

"Hadi!"

"I'm listening!"

She read: "The first time I was ever on an airplane was in 1955 and flights had names. This one was 'The Golden Gate,' American Airlines. Serving Transcontinental Travelers between San Francisco and New York . . ."

She paused for a reaction she did not get. That third helping of paneer makhani had been two past too many.

"Did you fall asleep?"

"No!"

He forced his eyes to open. Behind her, dark shimmering leaves, outlined against an impossible blue. Her shadow over him would have offered a brief respite from the light, if she would hold still.

"I was listening! She was on a plane—"

"That's not the point!"

She just couldn't hold still, could she?

"Flights had names! Not numbers, names! How utterly magical is that?"

Magical, a Sama word. She was practically effervescent.

"How come you never read books in Arabic?"

She seemed not to hear. She read on:

"The next summer I went back on 'The New Yorker,' United Airlines, and had a Martini-on-the-Rocks and Stuffed Celery au Roquefort over the Rockies . . ."

She let herself swoon back onto the grass and moaned:

"I want a Martini-on-the-Rocks and to be on a flight somewhere . . . I don't think you're allowed to fly in the third trimester."

He rolled his eyes behind closed lids. Maybe if he kept really still . . . but no, of course. She said:

"If you were a flight, what would you be named?"

He hated these games. He was terrible at these games. It was too hot for these games. There had been too much cream and hot chili in that paneer.

"I don't know, Sama . . ."

The Syrian government had conducted two chlorine attacks in less than two weeks: one bomb on Saraqeb, one on Aleppo. Hadi was going to be a father. Hadi was still reeling from the image of the brown-eyed girl, who could not have been more than four, whose eyes were bloodshot like a cocaine addict's, over an oxygen mask, which kept sliding because she was mothering her little brother. He was trying to remove his mask. They had the same eyes, big and round and curving slightly at the side like walnuts, but his irises were lighter.

Now Sama propped her elbows onto his belly. He winced and felt his lunch move quite the wrong way. Her nose scrunched at him. It was starting to peel. Her lower lip curled. She said, "Fine, I'll give you an easier one. If you could fly anywhere, right now, where would you go?"

"Well," Hadi snapped, "that depends. In this la-la world of yours, would I need a visa?"

It came out more bitter than he had intended but seemed to ease the heartburn. And there was more of it.

"I don't think too many exotic places are welcoming Syrians with open arms these days. Or have I magically turned into one of your birds, or an American?"

She was too stunned to speak at first. They both were.

"What's wrong with you?"

"I can't go anywhere, Sama!"

"I was just playing—"

"There are people dying at home, Sama! And you're just playing!"

The sunglasses stayed on. She sat up and closed the book and was quiet and looked straight ahead at the children running through the sprinklers. An actual breeze, faint but real, had picked up from the west. Speckled shadows of chestnut leaves danced on her, trickling down her neck and shoulders and the book's blue leather cover.

"I should take this back to the library."

He had married the most beautiful girl in the world, he thought. Sunlight caught on the thin gold band on her finger. It had been just the two of them the day he slipped it on. And a clerk with a stained blue tie, no photos or family. Just the two of them, alone in a wild wide world, and now . . .

"I'll meet you at the apartment. I just have to finish that chapter for Mendelssohn—"

"I'm sorry."

He touched her arm.

He sat up and placed his other hand tentatively on hers. She did not remove it. They watched the children, soaked and squealing, be lured away, to the gelato shop across the street. He opened his mouth to say *I love you* and said, "Let's get gelato."

Because she loved gelato. He could barely move, barely breathe, and would never eat Indian food again, at least for a month, but she loved gelato, fior di latte and nocciola in a cone.

"Then I'll walk you to the library?"

She nodded.

*   *   *

The queue outside the shop wrapped itself around the corner. He was melting and held her hand. Her wedding band was cool.

He said, "So where would you go?"

He could see only the chin crumple, then the smile. The queue snailed on as she thought. Finally, she said, "I'd go everywhere. I'd keep flying around the world and never land."

SAMA

"Naseem."

I look at him, asleep in his purified world.

"It means light breeze," I tell the nurse, and taste the name in its entirety: "Naseem Deeb."

The syllables flow off my tongue, limpid, rustling through trees, rippling over seas and fields and sand dunes. *Naseem . . .*

We had wanted a name as clear and vast as this country, his by birth, ours by choice, by wish, by need, by hope. A name he could breathe, but also one he could stand on. A heritage. A name that smelled of earth, the budding citrus of our fathers' orchards, the nutmeg of our mothers' kitchens. A name that recalled the country you and I had come from.

"It's a lovely name," the nurse says. "I'll bring you a birth certificate form. You will need the father's signature too. Have you been able to reach him?"

HADI

Y*ou have reached Jeffries and Associates, attorneys at law. We're
sorry we missed your call. Please leave a message with your name and
contact information and we will get back to you as soon as possible.
We strongly advise against discussing the details of your case with
anyone but—"*

"*You have reached the American embassy in Amman. Our normal
business hours are . . ."*

"*You have reached Jeffries and Associates, attorneys at law. We're
sorry we missed your call. Please—"*

". . . Hello?"

His voice. *His* voice. I break into sobs.

"Hello? Who is this?"

I cough and wheeze. The words won't come, just waves, one
after the other, of racking fear.

"Who is this?" he asks again.

"It's Hadi Deeb . . ."

I gasp between waves.

"My God! Hadi! I've been calling you since yesterday! Where
are you?"

I hold on to the phone like a life buoy.

"Hadi, where are you? Answer me!"

TRAVEL BAN CAUSES CHAOS, HUNDREDS DENIED ENTRY

Over the past forty-eight hours, the travel ban has left refugees, immigrants, and visitors with valid visas stuck in legal limbo.

The executive order, issued on the 27th of January and banning travel to the US from seven Muslim-majority countries, has caused major confusion at the nation's airports as some people from those countries were detained as they arrived in the US. Customs and Border Protection (CBP) reported that 721 people were detained or denied boarding.

When I am finished, two silences. Paul's is opaque. Mine drowns in the roar of the human tide exiting Amman Airport. Exodus. Arrivals. Elbows knock me around. Bodies and announcements whirl in Arabic, in English.

"Paul?"

Nothing. Not even Paul Jeffries breathing. I haven't heard him silent since we met.

"I'm here."

I almost look for his face in the crowd. His broad shoulders, broad smile, robust pink face, the first real American face I saw. I almost look for the sign he held with my name in English and, underneath, in some strange string of letters he must have meant as Arabic. My name. There are some signs with names in English here. No one is waiting for me here.

"Paul . . ."

This time it's a plea. *Paul, don't leave me here.*

His words slice through the silence: "Do you have the form?"

"What?"

"The form! The damn form they made you sign! Do you have it?"

"Yes. They gave it back to me on the plane."

"Read it to me."

Clumsily, I pull the paper from my coat. It takes precious minutes to unfold.

"Come on, son!"

The first line is in blaring bold letters.

"TO BE COMPLETED BY ALIEN WHEN APPLICATION FOR ADMISSION WITHDRAWN:

"I understand that my admissibility is questioned for the above reasons . . . which I have read, or which have been read to me in the ENGLISH language. I request that I be permitted to withdraw my application for admission . . ."

I pause, but nothing.

". . . and return abroad. I understand that my voluntary withdrawal . . ."

I read the text to its end. The silence that follows is damning. Then, in a whisper I barely hear:

"Hadi. You shouldn't have signed it . . ."

It is my turn to shout:

"I didn't have a choice! They said if I didn't sign, I would be barred from reentering the US for five—"

"They lied," he says with such calm conviction that I want to punch a wall. I heave against his tone, bolt out from under it. I am angry at Paul for the cool, hard— Then I hear the words. *They lied.*

They lied?

Something shatters in my head. Something I believed unbreakable, believed in all my life, staked my life on. I left Syria on that belief, I promised it to my parents. It carried me that awful night in Douma. I trusted . . .

Suddenly, the ground under my feet feels tenuous, shaky.

"Hadi, are you there?"

But I can only breathe.

His voice is softer: "Okay, it's okay. We'll figure it out. Give me a minute to think. It's okay."

In that minute, I stare at the form and don't see it. I see the years of other forms I signed: the applications, questionnaires, statements, and pledges, and lines and lines of dotted lines. Paul's face at

Logan Airport, larger and brighter and more Technicolor than all the pictures I ever saw of Times Square.

Paul speaks cautiously: "Well, the good thing is that the whole country's up in arms. Protests, the media, organizations filing lawsuits. Some judges are trying to block the order, although I don't know if—"

He stops.

"What time is it in Jordan?"

I look at the phone.

"One thirty-four a.m."

"Get in a cab, go to a hotel, get something to eat, call me from there."

His voice nonnegotiable. I want to hide in that voice.

"I'll work on a plan."

Something lifts, something that had been colossally heavy. In its place, something soft I can breathe through.

"Thank you."

"And Hadi?"

I hear the burly man shuffle.

"I'm sorry about your father."

The tears finally come.

He turns the meter on before we move, before he even asks, "*Oustaz,* where would you like to go?"

I almost laugh. Where would I like to go? Back to baggage claim. At least there everyone was in limbo. I wasn't the only one in no-man, no-country land, watching the belt turn, Russian roulette merry-go-round, waiting for my bag, which didn't come. Of course it didn't arrive. Only I did, here. Wherever the hell "here" is.

"*Oustaz?*"

"I don't know!" I yell at the plastic wall between the driver and me, for lack of another target.

Stifled, I turn to open the window. There is no crank.

"How do I roll down the window?!"

"It's broken, *Oustaz* . . ."

I yank open the door of the beat-up Mercedes and hurl myself out.

Sky, too dark, but not enough for stars. Too many streetlights, dirty mustard, and the airport's, blinding white. But at least air. I gulp it in. Not enough.

Where would you like to go? They didn't ask, and it's far too late now, *Oustaz*. You can't ask that question of a man with no suitcase and nothing left.

SAMA

The journey in reverse, from the tenth floor to the fifteenth, is brutally short. Crash-landing into the room. Crystal blue through the large window. Screamingly empty, obscenely bright. I have misplaced my husband, and my son has never seen sky.

"What would you like to do now?" asks the nurse, with the trained upbeat tone of all professional caregivers. "Have some breakfast? We could—"

"Shower, please."

At least in the bathroom I can shut the door and make it dark. She hands me a towel.

There is no lock on the bathroom door. I need one, desperately. I need the safe, solid click of a bolt sealing me in. I push the stool against the door. I begin to undress. Bruises. Flaps of skin sag; yesterday they were taut. Flakes of blood—not all of it mine—in the folds. The mesh underwear is soaked.

Sliding it down to my ankles is so painful, I gasp. Air hurts. Sight hurts. I switch the lights off and shower in the dark. Water hurts. I never would have thought that water could hurt. But I welcome its pressing, scalding heat. Touch, any. Feeling. I let it flow with the water, burn my neck, my spine, my legs till it reaches the drain. The blood must be tinting the tiles pink, scarlet, vermilion.

A sharp pain in my breasts. A drop of something thick at the tip of each nipple. *Milk* . . . My body begging for contact with the baby it knows exists. *Where is my baby?* I don't know what to tell it. Where is my husband? Where are the friends, the sunny streamers, the presents?

I vomit . . . nothing: bile, pain. Still retching, I turn the knob for hotter water. It will not go farther.

The nurse has left a change of clothes on the bed: new gown, same blue. New beige socks and mesh underwear. All of it disposable. Next to the anonymous uniform, she also set my phone. Dozens of missed phone calls and messages. *Are you okay? Have you seen the news?* The phone lights up in my palm.

"Hadi! Where are you?"

*. . . **h**is campaign speech, he called for a total and complete shut-down, saying, 'We can't allow people coming into this country who have this hatred of the United States' . . ."*

"Sama!" Hadi called, shouting over the television. They had a television now, and a wall to hang it on. "Your tea is getting cold!"

He knocked on the door, and found her on the blue tiles, hugging the toilet bowl.

He sank down next to her and held her hair. She was, profusely, sick again.

Outside, "*. . . they have this great hatred of Americans!*"

"The cannoli were a mistake," she managed, just, and had to hurl again.

A few seconds later, between shallow breaths, mortified by the scene before them, she said, "I'm so sorry, Hadi. I'm sorry I made you go out and get them. No more cannoli for the pregnant lady."

He pushed the hair off her damp forehead and said solemnly, "You can have all the cannoli in the North End. Just maybe not for breakfast."

She gave him a pale smile. He pulled her up, steadying her until the heartburn passed and the swaying floor under her feet solidified. She felt disgusting, she said. She looked incandescent, he thought. They walked out, his arm around her waist. Protests on the screen. Too loud. He muted the screaming faces but kept the TV on. She made more tea while he read the headlines streaming in bold red letters across the bottom of the screen.

"Is it Syria?" she asked as she sat down, then gasped. Immediately Hadi turned the TV off.

She had already seen. The long, snaking line of men, boys, some with zombie faces, on the black, white-lit tarmac, hands behind their backs . . . disappeared into a black screen. She burst into tears.

"Sama! *Hayati!* Don't cry!"

"They all look like you . . ."

Hadi sighed. His face was dark. "This guy wants to deport half the people in this country as soon as he's sworn in . . ."

She went paler than post-cannoli, and he spoke quickly: "Not us, Samati. Not us."

SAMA

Executive Order 13769: By the authority vested in me as President . . .'"

"Don't read it to me, Hadi! Tell me what it means!" I shout at the phone, at the large window, at the sky, painfully blue. It is still day here, and there is not a cloud, and at first, your words evoke nothing. Then, slowly, horrifyingly, they darken into scenes.

Flashes, news flashes. Headlines we saw on TV, last year, last month, just last week. *Zero tolerance! Build a wall! Deported.* Words, just words drowning me. Your words: *not us.* The looping videos. *Their* drowning eyes, those boys, handcuffed, lined up like cattle. Every one of them has your face. Every headline now reads *Hadi.*

"They released the order on Friday. Section 3(c) blocks entry into the US of all visa holders from Iran, Iraq, a number of other countries, and of course Syria, for at least ninety days."

"But that doesn't apply to you! You're a refugee!"

"Section five," you continue, as though you had not heard, as though you were sitting across from me, reading the paper, "suspends all refugees for at least one hundred and twenty days, and Syrian refugees indefinitely."

In the silence that follows, in the air, I see the headlines again. People and their lives reduced to thin layers of ink on flimsy paper. The deceit of words on a page. Our own, skimming them, stirring tea, from a safe, surgical distance, barricaded from seeing.

I see everything now, distinctly. Every line on your face. Still, stupidly I ask:

"What do you mean, 'indefinitely'?"

No response.

"But . . . you're already here! You live here. You have a wife and—"

Not now. Not like this.

"And besides, where would you go? It's not like they can send you back to Syria . . ."

There is a silence I only heard once, the night it rained bombs and glass on our heads in Syria. More of a whistle, like a kettle, so loud it shouldn't be called silence. Steam burning your ears deaf. You were the only person who ever nodded when I described it. You did not answer the first time I asked: "Hadi? Where are you?"

HADI

Nowhere. Some room in some hotel, some taxi drive from the airport. Walls, carpets. Beige. Functional, bluntly thrifty. Adequate, forgettable, for adequately forgettable travelers in transit.

Except I'm not in transit.

"*He's a real nowhere man, sitting in his nowhere land . . .*" I sing, finding the minibar. *Yil'aan abouhon.* Empty. "*Making all his nowhere plans . . .*"

"Hadi? Are you singing?!"

Hayati, you introduced me to Lennon. What did I know about the Beatles? What did Lennon know about nowhere? Fucking Lennon and his British passport and fucking platinum records.

"Are you drunk?!"

"Ha! I wish. There's nothing to drink in this *khara* hotel. And the restaurant's closed. I would kill someone now for a Big Mac."

"Hadi . . ."

"But hey, they gave me a toothbrush! And a razor! Did I tell you my suitcase didn't arrive?"

Suddenly, it's hilarious. Howlingly hilarious. Pound-my-fist-into-the-fucking-thin-plaster-wall hilarious.

"Hadi . . ."

Sorry, Sama. I can't stop.

"Let me tell you what did arrive."

All I have I splay out on the table.

"Wallet, useless. Passport too, except as a memento, I guess. And of course, Form I-275."

I unfold it again. The creases are firmly marked now and beginning to brown. It must be the heat. My Boston coat is hanging on a chair.

"'I understand that my voluntary . . .' Ha, I signed under 'voluntary.' You know what this form doesn't specify, Sama? That the alien has to pay for his own return ticket. Isn't it hilarious? You only find out after. Smart *ikhwan sharameet*. They made me pay for my own deportation!"

I'm howling. I can't help it. I'm starving. Maybe I'll eat my passport, the fucking stubs of boarding passes: *two* layovers. The only ticket I could afford. It's so hot in here.

"Hadi . . ."

The window won't open!

"The fucking window won't open! What? Are they afraid I'll jump? From the second floor? You can't die if you jump from the second floor!" I shout at the glass.

"No one's that stupid! No one's that . . ."

The sobs come. *Stupid, or desperate.* You let me cry. On the bed, a bed, nowhere, till I drain the room of air.

Quiet. Breathing. Crying breathing. Not mine.

"Sama? *Allo?*" My voice echoes across the line, across . . . I cannot bear to think of the immensity of the space it travels. The sky is moonless here, and black. Where are the stars?

"Sama? Please."

Don't leave me here alone.

"I'm here. . . ."

"Why didn't you call?"

You said it so quietly. Still, it rang like glass.

"I . . . What do you mean?"

"From the airport, why didn't you call? Before they put you on the plane. They must have let you make a call."

I lie. "They didn't let me."

Through the crack in the window I managed to open, a hissing draft slips in. I slam the window shut. I have never lied to you before. Your husband is a liar, Sama. A lying coward, but you cannot hear my thoughts. I cannot hear yours, but you say nothing, and I realize you already know. And for one horrible moment, I have trouble picturing your face.

"I'm sorry, Sama. I'm sorry. Don't cry. It'll be okay."

Nothing. I ramble on, flooding the gaping chasm with promises.

"We'll be fine, Samati. It'll be okay."

Trying to reach you, put my hand on your arm, on the couch in our living room, but this void is too immense.

"Are you okay? And the baby? Where are you now, at home?"

Silence.

". . . Sama?"

SAMA

And just like that, we crossed the planet. Somewhere over the Atlantic, we touched.

"I have a son?"

"You have a son."

In a moment, shorter than a Planck, infinite, bursting with light. It swells, shimmering, filling every atom of space. And nothing else matters. All of it dissolves. Passports and CANCELED – BOS, planes and windowless rooms and little bits of boarding passes. Form I-275 and executive orders. Flimsy, vaporous documents. They blow away in glittering particles.

"My God, Sama. I, *bhebbik*."

I forget the words in English too.

"*Bhebbak*."

Bhebbik, you say again and again, like music notes beating in perfect cadence, certain like coming home. Like a heartbeat, like you are beating yours to me.

"*Bhebbak*," I tell you, beating my own across the planet and time, over walls and oceans. I don't know where they touch, but they do.

"Describe him to me?"

"I couldn't see him well in the incubator."

"It doesn't matter, Sama."

You're right. It doesn't. All right then, we take off, the three of us. I describe lashes that curl like petals. A nose, like yours. Ten fingers, almost impossibly fine. Ten toes. You ask for more, blind and starved. I describe almond eyes, the color of the sky at noon in July. On cheeks, freckled constellations. A dimple, same side as mine.

I describe the most beautiful baby. I tell us a story. I stretch it like sky from Boston to Amman. We both leap for it, hanging on, to the phone, to the words, as unconcerned with their truth as with gravity and the laws of men and nature. Reality and its ugly abysses and walls. I close my eyes and they cannot enter. Only light does. And in the space behind my eyelids, only the present: dabs of whites, blues, infinite blues, powder pinks and pastel greens.

I open my eyes and land us all safely. You, me, and Naseem. The birth certificate form is by the bed and pink.

"Will you fill out the birth certificate with me?"

The sound waves quiver in my ear. Babas shouldn't cry. Rather, when they do, the spinning earth should stop.

Ballpoint pen. First question:

"Child's full name: Naseem Deeb."

I wait for you to confirm. An exhale reaches me.

"It's perfect. It's . . ."

Air. Freedom. Our son's name is our dream. The greatest accomplishment of our lives. *Naseem Deeb*, American. Naseem Deeb, who will never be stopped by Customs and Border Protection.

"Mother's name, father's name, date and place of birth."

Naseem, son of Sama and Hadi, born on the twenty-eighth of January, in Boston, Massachusetts. Free to go wherever he wants, beyond all seas, all frontiers, all countries, be whoever he wants to be. Nothing and no one will trap Naseem.

In blue ink, I make the first indelible marks of the infinite that will draw him. I can already see, just as indelibly, that dazzling mosaic. Our son will have a deep-blue passport with a proud golden eagle. Naseem will have the life we came here for. I sign the form and date it.

For a moment, we stay there, in that swelling, shimmering space, then I ask:

"What do we do now, Hadi?"

I hear, almost feel, the exhale, warm and soft and long on my cheek. Take your time. I will wait. Here, with Naseem, on the other side of the world, vast and beautiful, we'll be here . . .

"All right, Sama, here's what we're going to do: Tomorrow, I'll call the embassy. Better yet, I'll just go there."

"Do you think they can help?"

"I have no idea, we'll see. There must be something they can do. I'll keep pestering them till they do."

"How long is your Jordanian visa valid?"

"A month. I have a few weeks left."

"You'll be back before then," I say, to you and me, and we believe it, like the color of Naseem's eyes.

August 2010

She would leave on Sunday night; the flight to Boston, through Paris, was cheapest then. Thus, the circumstances of lives altered; decisions made, part chance, part volition. Sama Zayat would leave Damascus on the first of August.

She would leave Syria and arrive in America the same day, very nearly at the same time, after a fourteen-hour, one-stop trip. It would be Sunday night there too, as though, as she flew, life would hold its breath and the world would pause its revolution. She would have time to find her luggage, her bearings. She would have weeks before orientation. She could, perhaps, have left on another Sunday, but there was no point in lingering. The decision had been made, long ago, a year ago on a Tuesday.

On a Tuesday one year ago, Mama blasted the window open over the kitchen sink, uncharacteristically; she was a mild woman and it was a mild evening. Like the bharat in the bamyeh, the trace of nuttiness in the lightly goldened rice with vermicelli. The breeze, dusty but temperate, blew from the west, clearing the kitchen of the last of the day's heat, and onion, rosemary, and garlic.

She began scrubbing the pots. Sama cleared the table and stood to her mother's right, ready with the towel. Baba remained on the stiff-backed Turkish pine chair, smoking his Gauloises. And something happened that altered the course of Sama's life.

Mama dropped a plate. It broke. The plate she broke was pink. It had been lilac, once, with crassly painted flowers in thick cyan. The colors had, for the most part, fortunately, faded, by the time Mama had inherited the set, missing a bowl and chipped. Sama hated it. She preferred the pure-white porcelain plates, silver rimmed, that the Zayats saved in the dining room for guests and special occasions. They saved the dining room for that as well.

Sama started and turned to her mother, just in time to glimpse something flicker across her face. Then her mother said:

"*Ya allah!* Look what I did!"

But Sama had already seen: Mama hated the plates too. She had never said so. Mama never said what she loved or hated, liked or did not like to eat. She had made bamyeh and rice that night, and warek 'einab stuffed with ground meat, tomatoes, parsley, no cilantro because Baba could not abide it. Mama owned gorgeous porcelain plates and never used them. She had bought them on a trip to Paris the summer before her wedding.

She contemplated the scatter of pink-and-blue debris across the beige ceramic tiles, a fraction of a second too long, then rushed for the broom and dustpan. She did not let Sama help. Two brush-strokes. The floor was beige again. She then returned to the pot and browned onion grime with zeal. She was going to scrub it raw.

"*Kahweh*, Wafi?"

"I'd love some."

"Sama, will you put the *rakweh* to boil?"

Mama had said she liked espressos, once, at a café near Bab Sharqi Street, whose owner brought back bags of Café Richard coffee every time he went to France. The two of them had babbled on and on in French, and he had excitedly offered Mama a bag of beans to take home. Next time, inshallah, she had said. She and Sama still had errands to run, but they would return. They had not. Mama had been seventeen when she married, Sama's age now. Eighteen when she had her.

Mama handed Sama the pot. It was slippery, like the unease Sama suddenly felt. It was too warm in the kitchen. Stifling, even. Damascene heat poured in through the window, dry, but she was sweating. The feeling trickled into her lungs, swelled, and was pressing out, leaving no room for air. There was no air in that kitchen.

"Baba, Mama, I got a scholarship."

Mama already knew. Mama had proofread the essays and sat by Sama's desk in the evenings, comparing programs, and late at night, on Sama's bed, whispering excitedly like she too was applying to Harvard. Mama knew, by now, more about admission rates and standardized tests, more vocabulary words than most Americans. She stopped scrubbing, nonetheless, but kept facing the sink.

Baba asked, "What scholarship?"

"To study in America, Baba. Harvard."

She drew a breath. Baba looked at her over his second cigarette. He let the ashes melt off the tip, then set the butt on the thick clay rim of the ashtray.

"You want to go to America?"

The floor felt porous under her feet. She looked down and caught a glimpse of one stray piece of broken pink, more a weak orange now from years of tomato and cumin. She could have done it better, at least differently, but too late; she had leaped. And it had to be said. It had to be said then. Now, fly or crash. Looking up, she continued:

"I want to study anthropology. I want to learn—"

"You want to study *what*?"

In Sama's head, pink plates shattered to magnificent bits.

There were shouts and there were tears. Accusations of folly, ingratitude, betrayal of her *ousoul*. Of him, whose own roots were a square of a corner shop near Souk Medhat Pasha, rented on borrowed money, selling potato chips and Alhamra cigarettes, and tepid bottles of Barada beer. Wafi Zayat, who spoke no English, then or now, who had built an empire—five Zayat stores, this apartment, two cars, the summer house in Mesyaf, with a vineyard and rose garden—for his wife and daughter, for her children, his grandchildren! He had built it all! He had provided, sheltered, loved . . .

But the louder Baba fought, the louder, higher, she pulled against those roots; they were dead weights, and she couldn't see the sky through his trees. They were blocking her escape. She would be seventeen next year. She needed freedom.

"Freedom from what?!"

His daughter, an immigrant! Nameless in a foreign country! She preferred the word *émigrée*. It sang. It felt airy, vowelly. She would be so: light and cosmopolitan, a world-touring saunterer, untethered by land or home, having shrugged both off, taking off, taking flight.

"*Majnouneh?!* What do you think America is? The crime, the drugs—"

She mutinied: "How on earth would you know that, Baba? You've never been!"

She could have stopped. She should have stopped. Mama was crying.

"How would you know anything about America? You've never even been on a plane! You've never been anywhere!"

Her voice lashed the air.

"Sama," her mother said.

"And you trapped Mama with you! Every year, you promise you'll take her to Paris!"

"Sama!"

"Sayde, it's all right."

It was the tone of his voice—low and hollow, quivering like he was just learning to speak—that knocked the air from her lungs. She crashed back into the kitchen, no, fell back, touching ground with the soft sound of a dead leaf. She saw what she had done.

Baba sat still, erect, swaying imperceptibly, as though his daughter's blows were still reverberating in him. He looked ahead, through her, past her, at Mama at the window, out the window onto the street. Blackened mountains. On one of those, a summer house and garden. She looked at him, carving every line, every curve and indentation of her father's face on her heart, wishing he would speak, silently begging him to. Realizing he wouldn't; she had punched the air from him too.

"Baba, I—"

"It's all right, Samati."

Samati. My Sama.

He was still looking at his wife.

"Sayde, I . . ." but he ran out of courage and Mama was still turned away, looking intently at the patterned tiles over the sink, or perhaps out the window. Silence, wafer thin, like jasmine petals. Lilac-veined, translucent. Only then did Sama smell the jasmine on the ledge. It had been wafting in all evening.

"I'm sorry, Sayde."

"Shh . . ."

Mama's voice blew the past away. Much else was said between them, but Sama could not hear it. Then Baba rose, and Mama put the *rakweh* on a low flame, on the gas stove.

No trumpets sounded. They had their coffee on the balcony, in three white thimble-size porcelain cups, hand-painted with sparse green and red strokes, on a tray Mama carried.

She was allowed one suitcase, twenty-three kilograms, and one carry-on bag. Whatever they would fit, she could take. She stared at the piles of clothes and books and letters on the bed, the chair, the floor, at the seventeen years of items and living she had gathered.

In the mirror on the wall, shy breasts and spindly legs, white shirtdress whose collar and skirt—pleat by careful pleat—Mama had ironed. And insisted she travel in, over Sama's protests. She would freeze on the plane, the pleats were sure to crease, but Sama Zayat would be the best-dressed immigrant to land in the US.

Best dressed, wide, wild doe-eyed. For a year, her eyes had been filled with anticipation and wonder: Harvard! America! An ebullition of sounds, textures, and aromas coloring living snapshots of lecture halls and libraries, walls of books and skyscrapers and redbrick buildings. And she, in that vision, landing in a white dress . . .

"*Yalla*, Sama? Ready?" Baba called from the living room. She was not ready.

Her eyes were not filled with wonder now. They were taking in the reflection of Damascus behind her. Roofs of naked cement, wires, antennas, minarets, domes, and satellite dishes at precarious angles. Gray and blue, sometimes red reservoirs, hopeful for rain. Not a chance. Not a breeze. A patch of sky, clear, in the window frame. Not a sign of rain.

Not a sign, beyond the pallor of her face, her dilated pupils, of the storm beating inside her ribs. In the mirror, the roof of her school, the old khan, Najla's bedroom across the street, on the second floor. By the bed, passport propped like a shrine; inside it, a visa.

No, she was not ready. She had said her goodbyes, had dinner, had not packed, had only a few hours until departure. She should not have waited till the last minute.

Mama had abruptly announced she couldn't help her pack. There was too much to do in the kitchen, which was, presently, quiet. Mama, for dinner, had made every single one of Sama's favorite dishes: labneh; mana'eesh, toasted on the gas stove, sesame sparkling in a glistening sea of zaatar and olive oil; tabbouleh; loubieh bi zeit; and gloriously creamy, syrupy, ashta-stuffed atayef. Sama had eaten four.

One loved as one knew how. Mama had offered food, and Sama, that night, had eaten plate after plate because she loved her mother. She had eaten to make amends to her mother for leaving, leaving so easily, leaving her in the kitchen to wash and dry the dishes. One could love endlessly, but one could also only love as one could; Sama could not stay, and Mama could no longer bring herself to enter the bedroom.

She wasn't scared. She was not scared. She was simply not ready. She had simply eaten one too many ashta atayef.

Baba entered her room then, looking suspiciously meek, carrying a suspiciously heavy basket.

"What is that?" she asked sharply.

"Zaatar, dried figs, apricots," he recited, looking in. Continued: "Nuts, rose water, two boxes of karabeej . . . Your mother knows how much you like them . . ."

The fear, just then, exploded into a tumultuous apogee.

"Baba! I have no room for all of this!"

"Take it up with your mother."

"I hate dried fruit! She knows that!"

"Dried fruit is good for you! You need fruit."

"They have fruit in America!"

But there was more! He unloaded the basket's remaining contents: Mama's cookbook, Mama's rosary, Mama's . . .

She burst into tears. She had only one suitcase. She was only seventeen. She had a terrible, paralyzing ache in her stomach. She had made a mistake. She could not stop crying, could not pack, could not go to America.

"There are rules, Baba! I only have twenty-three kilograms!"

It wouldn't fit, her life: the books and dresses, scarves, diaries, faces that made up her past. Mama's lapis earrings. Baba, how old would he be when she saw him next? The gaping, terrifying emptiness outside . . .

Without warning, Baba crossed the enormous space between them; a few steps, three at most, the length of outstretched arms. He took her in his, and she cried in his shirt, gulping in his cologne, lemon and verbena, memorizing it. Soaking up the heat emanating from his chest. He held her till her heartbeat paced itself to his, then pulled away and said:

"It's okay, *ya zghireh.*"

Little one.

"It will fit."

And to her surprise, everything did. All her seventeen years, and the karabeej and zaatar, the rosary. She left the rose water. She would wear the earrings. Baba zipped the suitcase shut. To be relieved or sad that this was all of it, her life in her homeland . . .

Mama said goodbye at the door, though she had her purse in her hands.

"I'll miss you," Sama cried.

"Do you have everything?"

"Yes, Mama."

From her purse, she took a wad of dollar bills held together by a fraying green rubber band. She shoved it into her daughter's hand. "Have something to eat when you arrive." Then she turned away and left, remembering, suddenly, something she had left on the stove.

Pity the abandoned. To leave is to leave behind. Things and people. Take. Off. Baba carried the twenty-three kilograms. Sama followed.

It is also unclear to scientists just how birds know exactly, and collectively it seems, when the time has come to leave. How, exactly, that pivotal moment is reached: changes in day length, temperature, hormones . . . What has been observed can best be described as a sort of restlessness, an innate pull out and up that, if birds were human and scientists prone to using such terms, almost looks like longing.

It has been observed that birds feel a sort of pain before taking off, almost like fear, and that nothing alleviates that feeling except the rapid motion of wings.

SAMA

I saw you, Hadi. I dreamt you were drowning. I watched you, like you were in an aquarium, being flogged by giant waves, banging against the glass. I banged from the other side. You opened your mouth to scream and, somehow, salt water filled my lungs. I woke up gasping and you weren't there, and I was gripping the bed's bars. It was salt water; my thrashing had yanked out the saline drip.

Something liquid trickles down my arm. Six a.m., green and fluorescent on the bedside table. Six a.m. Boston dark is not molten, Damascus dark; it glitters. Outside Room 1508, the glass skyline, the Charles. One white, flashing light crowns the Hancock like a star. Beacon Hill, burgundy Beacon Hill, is still deep mauve.

A knock.

"May I come in?"

Dr. Farber. Wet hair, clean scrubs; she went home last night. My heart sinks and sees a kitchenette, blue Ikea plates on a sail-white counter, a dinner I will have to throw out when—

"I hope you slept well. I just saw your son."

My heart leaps.

"You saw Naseem? How is he?"

She hesitates, not long, just long enough to stop my next breath.

"Ms. Zayat, your— Naseem was stable overnight. No sign of jaundice, which is good."

She pauses, as do I, midair.

"But his blood pressure is still too low, and his temperature keeps dropping, even in the heated incubator."

She seems to be dispensing the information piecemeal, like bits of bread to a bird.

"There could be many reasons for hypotension: blood loss during delivery, an infection, a cardiac complication . . . It could also be because it took so long for him to breathe when he came out."

Break. Maybe she hears the frenzied flapping in my ears.

"I must remind you, Ms. Zayat, that the chances for babies born this early . . ."

Boston, this early, still glittery.

". . . started him on pressors and will be monitoring closely for new symptoms—"

Dr. Farber stops midsentence and looks at me. I don't know what she sees, but she says, "Why don't we go see him?"

Too many, too many wires and tubes, too soon for a child. Too dark in this room for a child. I used to be scared of the dark.

Babies should be laid on their backs to reduce the risk of suffocation. I used to sleep on my stomach, hands and feet and covers tucked in, every crevice sealed, cocooned, so the dark of the room wouldn't enter.

I would wait for the soft swish of Mama's slippers, reassuring me that the floor still existed. Wait for her hand on my back, through the covers, then she would sing . . .

Tiri ya tiyara, tiri . . .

The words I did not know I remembered flow into my head. It has been years since that lullaby, years since I sang in Arabic, since I thought in Arabic; the words sounded wrong in my head. Like they didn't belong to the Sama who came to the US. They sound perfect now, in this room. I lean over the incubator. Through the plastic wall:

Tiri ya tiyara, tiri, ya warek wa khitan
Fly off, fly, paper plane and string,
I want to be a child, on the neighbors' roof, again,
and have time forget me there.

He does not stir.

"That's lovely. Is that Arabic you're singing?" Dr. Farber asks.

"Yes, I'm from Syria."

"I've been there."

I look at her in surprise. She smiles and her cheeks turn a soft pink.

"Damascus, Aleppo, beautiful cities. I went there just before the war began. The music, the spices . . . I remember this one souk, even the air tasted of spices there."

I watch her return there with an ease I envy.

"I suppose it's quite different now."

I nod. Different.

"Do you have family there?"

"My parents live in Damascus."

"Is that where your husband is?"

The answer sticks in my throat, dry as the sumac in Souk al-Hal, not the souk she would have visited. Foreigners visit Al-Hamidiyah. For the second time today, I am envious of Dr. Farber, this woman who can go places like Damascus, Aleppo, return home to a place in Boston . . .

I turn to Naseem and continue to sing:

'Alli fo' stouh b'aad, 'a nasmeh el khajouleh,
Akhadouni ma'ahom el welad wa raddouli el toufouleh
Over distant roofs, on a timid breeze,
The children took me off with them . . .

The notes trill and flit. There is music inside the words.

If only we could run away, fly off on that paper plane,
It is too soon to grow up still.
Let the pomegranate blossoms sway in the orchards,
That the children may play . . .

We should go now. Dr. Scott will want to examine you before going over your discharge papers."

My heart bolts and beats, too loud. I choose not to understand.

"But Naseem can't leave yet."

Dr. Farber does not speak. The beat loudens. I should have left my heart outside. I should have known better than to let it in yesterday.

"I'm not leaving without my son!"

My son. The words are real, searingly real. Now look at this mess.

"Ms. Zayat," Dr. Farber says, cautiously choosing her words. "Naseem will probably be here awhile—"

"How long?" I interrupt.

She does not reply.

"A few days? A week? A month? How long until he can come home?"

She gives me a strange look. The word *home* ricochets. A doctor should never leave a mother's question in the air.

"I'm not leaving him alone!"

"He won't be alone. His monitors are on, and the nurses check in every hour—"

"Every hour?!"

Horrifying possibilities rise and swell: What if something happens and no one is there? What if he cries? What if he's afraid? What if I am? Paralyzed. My heart seals itself to the incubator wall, my feet to the floor. I could no sooner leave than fly, than the earth break out of orbit.

"Ms. Zayat, he's in good hands, I promise. He'll be fine."

I shake my head. I cannot shake the ton of steely fear off my chest. Dr. Farber does not understand.

"You can visit Naseem every day, then go—"

"Where?"

Where do I go?

"Go home! Sleep in your own bed."

Again, I shake my head. She doesn't understand.

"It's empty."

The bed, the home, and dark. And how do I tell Naseem, how do I tell my heart I'll be back, so they can hear me? I hide my face to cry. I used to believe that if I closed my eyes, the dark would not see me either.

Something touches my shoulder. A silver wedding ring. A smell of soap, unscented, just clean. I breathe it in and think *just a feeling, just a feeling.* You used to say that when you woke up from your dreams. The terror does not disappear, but ebbs. I look up and am in the neonatal ICU again. Dr. Farber removes her hand.

"Sama, I can't order you to go home, but you've got . . . a long road ahead of you. You *must* rest. I know you're scared—"

"He's all alone!"

"He's not, and neither are you. Rest. We'll take care of him so that when he's ready to leave, you can take over."

She said *when*. She said *when*. A slip of the tongue, probably, but oh, how fragile, fleeting, sudden, and powerful, that thing with feathers. It fills my lungs like a skyful of mountain wind and calms my heart. Dr. Farber sees and nods.

"Do you want to say goodbye to your son? Tell him you'll be back?"

I look at the boy who has my heart and contemplate the universe of words, in Arabic, English, French, all the languages I know and don't. They swirl and melt on my tongue. Cotton candy, strands of clouds. White and blue. Powder blue, like his eyes, which I have never seen open. Like the eyes of all children when they are born, regardless of their citizenship.

"I love you," I mouth, in English, in Arabic, in every language and with every atom in me.

"Ready?" Dr. Farber asks.

I follow her out anyway.

August 2010

The sliding doors shut behind her. Silently. Thunderously. Even as the plane had been landing, it had not seemed possible. Even as, eyes to the window, in that hazy state between sleep and wake, time zones, land and air, she had watched the lights approach, sparkle, swell . . .

Sama Zayat had flown.

She had flown before, many summers ago, from a tree. She had been four or five, and at the family house in Mesyaf. There had been pear trees, roses, trellises of vines, but also worlds and worlds of pine forests. She would climb over the fence, run off, disappear for hours, return, knees muddied, dress blissfully in tatters. It terrified Mama.

The day she got lost, they found her, by twilight, up in a tree, not scared—she did not know what that meant. From below, Baba bellowed; Mama cried. They looked so different.

Everything looked different: the last bursts of light and sky through the needles and the twigs . . . so beautiful she announced—in all seriousness, so Mama says—that she was going to become a bird.

She told them, calmly, that she was going to fly away, and climbed to the highest branch . . .

Touchdown. They had landed. Sama Zayat was seventeen and had flown over the Atlantic.

Arrival! Just as she read the word, an invisible force thrust the crowd forward, like a giant wave, sweeping Sama along. It was an emotion, palpable, more overwhelming even than takeoff had been. A feeling, like a dipping roller coaster. No, magnified, sublime.

They flew through the doors, to the carouseling luggage. One was hers to claim, like the country waiting outside. Her soles burned; her eyes flitted. Her suitcase was black, unlabeled. It took some time to locate.

She had not anticipated the sea of other unmarked suitcases and people. The buzzing in her ears: English! People speaking in English! In variegated, brightly colored, rising and falling accents. People speaking French, Spanish, Russian, Vietnamese . . . exotic, incomprehensible, intoxicating. Swarming her senses. A delicious, welling blend of anonymity and communion.

No one looked like her, or at her, or would recognize her when she walked through those last doors. She was foreign in a sea of foreigners; tourists, immigrants, exiles, home-comers; in a country she could only glimpse in her mind, pink, gold. Into which she could dissolve but would remain insoluble, whole. So this was freedom: the possibilities of becoming.

Behind baggage claim, a sign, regal, in pink and orange neon:

DUNKIN' DONUTS

Her heart flapped madly in her chest. Columbus must have felt this. This split-second feeling after a leap, onto a wave of air. There were Dunkin' Donuts in Syria, but this one was here, in America! She wished her Mama could see it.

She took out the roll of dollars her mother had given her and walked up to the counter.

She had never had a donut, and in Syria, she had rarely, if ever, eaten alone. But she was not in Syria. And she didn't know if she liked donuts. She ordered one, sugar-glazed, and a small black coffee.

Sama ate her first meal in the United States, alone, slowly, on her feet, at a tall and round steel table ringed with traces of past coffees. The texture, in her mouth and of the moment, was light, soft, unfamiliar. Exhilaratingly sweet.

She watched herself from a distance, in her wrinkled dress. Sugar rush. She could be anyone. Final bite. Sama Zayat was a person who liked donuts.

"Sama Zayat?"

Short, stout. Prominent nose. Thick, coarse, cindered hair. Thin round gold-rimmed glasses. He looked like Baba, she thought. No, he looked nothing like Baba. Except for the mustache. She could not imagine Baba in tweed, could not imagine him at Harvard.

"Did I pronounce it right?"

He sounded nothing like Baba. His voice was softer, deep, like pipe tobacco, with an accent she could not place. Crisp *k*s and *t*s, counterbalanced by gentle sshing *s*s. A hesitation, a half breath before he spoke. She had noticed it several times, interspersed in his lecture.

He had not looked as she entered, for which she had been grateful. He had simply carried on with the lesson, allowing her to slip into the nearest empty seat. She had not spoken, not dared look up from her desk until class had been dismissed.

Now the desks were empty, and she nodded.

"Yes, Sama Zayat"—newly alighted on campus, in America, and twenty enormous, mortifying minutes late to his lecture.

"I'm so sorry. I got lost." Her English thick on her tongue, an ailment she had only recently contracted; Sama had an accent. It had appeared soon after arrival.

Professor Mendelssohn looked up and now, at her. A ray of light got caught in his glasses and glinted.

"I have been teaching this class in this same classroom for decades. I still get lost. Every semester someone shows me again."

Crow's-feet materialized.

"Where I come from, everything is very small."

He did not say where that was or ask where she was from. The first person not to since she had landed in America.

Sama had an accent. Sama spoke English—or had thought she did—well. She had attended an American school in Syria, watched

American television, read American books, danced to American songs on Friday nights that had ended in American drive-thru restaurants. She had craved America, had thought she knew America, had taken off, and landed.

Professor Mendelssohn asked, "How is your semester going so far?"

At orientation, she had gripped her lemon seltzer while witty quips crisscrossed the air over her head, sparking guffaws, slaps on backs, the clinking of cans and glasses. America had an accent—and it was strong. Slang and a sense of humor she could not decode. America spoke and dressed and sounded foreign. Except she was the foreigner. She felt like an explorer who had stumbled upon an obscure tribe. She had stood at the fringe and laughed whenever the others had, tossing her head back, vaguely dizzy. A heady sort of lightness.

Like stepping off a ledge, into a whirlpool of words, swirling so fast they blurred.

"Are you enjoying your classes?"

She realized she had not answered the professor's first question. She nodded, too emphatically.

"It's very . . . different."

They, Sama, not *it*! She bit her tongue. *That* was why she had stopped raising her hand during lectures! She had no idea how to manipulate this language, navigate this maze of granite hallways, oak desks, and she was all alone and an idiot.

But then Professor Mendelssohn looked at her and said, "It is," and from behind his glasses, something cut through the clear, hard wall she had been knocking against.

"It takes . . . time," the older man said, enunciating, his own accent mild but unashamed and distinct. His English sounded earthier than an American's, but somehow, his words were easier to understand.

"Everyone here is trying to find their place, even those students who seem most confident. I noticed you did not take part in the discussion at the end of the lecture."

"I—"

"I hope you will next time. I'm sure you have much to say."

She wasn't sure, she wanted to tell him, of anything. She was very far from home and very separate.

"My English—"

"Can only get better," he said, ticking his *t*.

SAMA

The ride from the hospital is jarring; the traffic lights and cars and pedestrians and world flowing past the window, carrying on, in everyday color, as though they had not stopped since Saturday. The taxi stops and I am not sure how I got here.

First foot on the ground. It wavers. The second almost gives out as I pull myself upright. My center of gravity has shifted to the back, a consequence of months spent carrying the promise of a baby. The lightness, now, is painful.

I drift unsteadily up the steps. Our names are on the buzzer, fourth button up on the left. I stare at them in disbelief, unscathed since Saturday. Not even a film of dust.

Hadi Deeb, Sama Zayat. Our names, still there, as is the brick facade with its blue door, four flights of steps, all creaky, some broken, to our apartment. I am back.

The smell of yesterday's paper in the entrance hall. I check the mailbox. Someone sent us a postcard. Tina and Frank are in Portugal. I discard the flyers and ads. I climb the stairs, lose my breath, fumble for the keys, already in my hand, climb the remaining steps to our door and hesitate. I do not want to enter.

As soon as I do, I trip on your shoes and burst into tears.

My cup of tea is right where I left it on Saturday evening. White porcelain, white countertop. The liquid inside it has dried, leaving an ugly ring of brown. The kitchenette and living room reek of soured hummus and limp greens. The rice on the stove has oozed out a thin film of white starchy liquid. The bread is hard. It crumbles in my fingers. The meat . . . I don't even look. I throw everything away and hurry to the windows. I open every last creaky white pane. Cold sun and cold air burst in. I never met the former tenants, who left only crescent-moon marks all over the old floorboards, relics of chairs dragged to and from the windows, close to and away from one another. The apartment had been empty when we moved in, scrubbed clean of the rest of its past. We ourselves did not own much, then or now. We brought our furniture with us. An Amazon-green sofa that, surprisingly, complements the lemon armchair we found by a dumpster, our "Positano" chair. Positano had been my dream, but Italy was not visa-friendly to Syrians, and besides, a weekend honeymoon in Florida had been closer, cheaper, lovely.

And Positano wasn't going anywhere, you said, and neither were we. And meanwhile, we had the armchair. My fingers graze the yellow fabric, rough and frazzled, of this chair someone abandoned in an alley. A harsh, cold yellow, or it might just be the icy blue of the light. I turn on the floor lamp. I turn on all the lamps.

Unhung prints of Chagall, Matisse. One of Degas's *Blue Dancers*. The set of Dutch blue hand-painted plates we rescued from a thrift shop. Piles of books on every surface, mine, including the floor—you would trip over them and curse—and the piano.

The piano. The best present in the history of presents, you said when you saw it and could finally speak. And the smooth, worn leather duffel bag stuffed with sheet music, which Mrs. Moore had thrown in too, at the last minute.

I stand in this museum of us. Without you, the objects seem disjointed and untethered, floating in the empty space, echoing against the walls, returning, unrecognizable to me. Only I am weighted down. The floorboards are cold under my feet.

Too cold, this room. I close the French windows. Too small now. The smell is still there. It is not the food.

Too enormous, this silence. Where is my phone? On the white, veined coffee table, that silly book you bought, the only one in here you did: a Lonely Planet guide, *Syria & Lebanon*. I suddenly understand. I'm so sorry I laughed.

The hours you spent in November, when it started getting dark at five, then four, reading descriptions—in English!—of places you already knew, marking the sights only tourists visit, combing the dog-eared pages for precise details, images.

I laughed. I am so sorry. I teased. I called your name, you didn't answer, and I was irritated. I didn't understand you couldn't hear. You weren't even in the room. In a place but not of it, you were missing home.

I almost call your name now, but no, no. You are already much too not-here. *Tiri ya tiyara, tiri*, away from here.

Across the ocean, on the other side of the line, I can almost hear the tinny notes of "La vie en rose." Mama's ringtone, Mama's relic of a phone. I know neither has changed since I left Damascus. I know the phone is on the marble table by the jade velvet sofa the sun has lightened. I know Baba is calling out, *Ya Sayde! Telephone!* I know she cannot hear him; she is chopping something in the kitchen.

"*Allo?*"

"Baba."

"Samati?"

Samati. The only other man in the world who calls me that. In an instant, lemon and verbena.

"*Weinik, ya binti?*"

I am five years old again and safe. I'm here, Baba. I'm here.

"You haven't called in days! *Sayde, ya Sayde! Taa'i!* It's Sama!"

"Sama? *Yalla, yalla! Jayi!*"

She places the knife on the board, wipes her hands hurriedly with the checkered kitchen towel that always falls off the hook. Even in her haste she will pick it up.

"*Yalla*, Sayde!"

The scuffle of slippers: French gray lined with fine lace.

Baba says, "Something smells wonderful."

"Warek 'einab."

His favorite. I hear a slap.

"Wafi! Stop eating those karabeej! The doctor said less sugar . . ."

"I didn't—"

"You have crumbs in your beard."

Now Mama has her hand on her hip and over Baba's beard, the two little telltale patches of cheekbone are pink.

"I only had one, *wallah*!"

And my heart suddenly aches for the sweet, powdery semolina, sticky pistachio paste, the hints of warid and orange blossom. My throat constricts.

"*Keifik, habibti?*"

"Fine, Mama, how are you?"

An almost-quiver as I force the lie out. She hears it, continents away.

"Sama? What's wrong, *habibti*?"

"Is everything all right?" Baba asks.

"Yes, everything is . . ."

I am crying. Scraped-knee-on-asphalt, bullied-in-the-playground crying. *Mama, Baba, please-mend-my-broken-five-year-old-world* crying. To my shame and horror, I cannot stop. The years of distance I built between us—in the name of freedom, my independence— collapse.

"Wafi, she's crying!"

"Samati, tell us what's wrong." His voice as far away and helpless as he.

"Ask her if she's sick! Did she eat?"

One loves as one knows how. Her questions cut across time.

"Your mother asks—"

"I ate," I lie, as all children do to the mothers they abandon. *Yes, I'm fine. No, I am not sick. A cold, allergies. Yes, of course I ate.* The transcripts of transatlantic phone calls are rife with lies, both ways; those we tell loved ones, those they tell us, all of which we believe, because we choose to, because they help us endure the distance.

"And I'm not sick. I'm . . ."

For a second I fantasize about one more lie:

The baby was born, premature but healthy. Don't worry, all is fine.

I imagine: *What did she say, Wafi? The baby, Sayde! He's here!* Silence for a moment, then a spring shower of *Mabrouk! Mabrouk, habibti!* Pastel, gossamer streams of blessings and congratulations.

"Well, then, what is it?"

My chin gives way and before I can stop it, the truth spills out, unfiltered. It gushes through the phone line, through the air, seven time zones, through the speaker, into my parents' salon. It breaks every rule every child knows not to when calling home. I finish and wait. Shell-shocked silence. Dust falling on still water.

Baba curses quietly: "*Yil'aan abouh*," so low it could have been a prayer. "*Yil'aan abouh . . .*"

"Wafi . . ."

"So he meant it. Every word he said in his campaign. The wall, the immigrants . . . *Yil'aan abouh. Yil'aan abouhon*, all of them."

The curses grow louder and deeper with his comprehension.

"*Yil'aan abouhon!* Them and their country! How dare they do this to people? To my daughter?"

The primal, bestial fury of a parent.

"We saw the news," Mama says, "but we didn't even—"

"Deporting people? A travel ban? They're a nation of immigrants, the hypocrites!"

"Baba."

But Baba cannot hear. He can only see his daughter, crying in a playground on the other side of a fence, a border, an ocean.

"*Yil'aan abouhon!*" As though said enough, loud enough, the words might match his anger, denounce, undo this injustice. They do not. They merely tire my father's smoker's lungs. He coughs, heaves, many minutes. His breathing finally slows. I wait for Baba to fix everything, as Baba always does.

He clears his throat.

"Where are you now? The baby . . ."

"I'm in the apartment. The baby's at the hospital."

"*Habibti*," murmurs Mama, and there is nothing else to be said, nothing that could bridge this giant gulf. Nothing to fix.

"Are you in the living room?"

"Yes."

"On the sofa?"

I join them there, on the softened velvet that once was jade. I close my eyes and my fingertips remember tracing stars and waves, running across the fabric, upstream, ruffling the threads. Touch. There should be a way, someday, for fingertips to touch through phones, through screens and windowpanes, and the plexiglass of incubator walls.

"Are you both all right? Are you being careful?"

"We're fine, *habibti*. We're fine. Don't worry about us."

The lies we tell those we love, because we love.

As long as I keep my eyes closed, we sit on the sofa, in the silence of their breathing. Beyond my eyelids, the real, vacuous living room will not have changed. Every item, now devoid of meaning, will still be in its place. That there will be no sign, nothing to bear witness to the fact that the world has gone mad, is absurd and grotesque. Only spoiled food, hardened bread.

"Are there still bread shortages?"

"Shh, *habibti*. Let's not talk about that now."

They too must have their eyes closed, their hands overlapped on the sofa.

"Tell us about the boy. Does he look like Hadi?"

Outside my parents' window, people are dying, for words they said or didn't or forgot or now deeply regret. Queuing outside embassies for visas. Queuing for everything: lentils, flour, rice. Yanking cash out of ATMs, pawning their grandmothers' watches, selling gold, going to bed fully dressed . . . but in my parents' mad world, and in mine, there is a room with powder-blue walls and green velvet that smells faintly of tobacco, lemon and verbena, and a wafting aroma of warek 'einab.

"Do you need money?" Baba asks. From a country at war. One loves as one knows how.

"Wafi, ask her if she had dinner."

Nine thirty p.m. Past midnight in Damascus and Amman. It is dark there, and in a windowless room on the tenth floor in Massachusetts General Hospital.

From my window, another lamp-lit living room across the street in a brick town house. It looks like a reflection, fourth floor up, except this apartment would be to the right. Except in that living room, over a sleek black leather couch, facing TV, there are two heads. One is nodding off and snapping up. Nine thirty-one. Moonlight, tonight, is particularly insolent and harsh.

Nine thirty-two. Still past midnight in Damascus and Amman. No one to call, there, here, in Boston, anywhere. What would I say? Still, I put the phone to my cheek, for the cool, plastic, material feel of possibility: that it might, just might ring.

Nine thirty-five and it does not, but my hand will not drop. The phone suspended, on the hope . . . Nine thirty-nine.

Phone and heart drop to the sofa without a sound. The fall should have made one. Nowhereness should have a sound, like a gavel, a slamming door, thunder. But no. Nine forty-four.

Suddenly, out of that nowhere, some evolutionary force:

Keys! Phone! Coat!

The pressure eases the second I open the door. Down and onto the street, I burst like a bird from a cage. Left, to the amber lights of the main road, toward the river. I gulp in wind, wet and cold. Not sharp enough. Right, past the Dunkin' Donuts, too painfully bright; too orange and pink, still; in it, life still unfolding too innocently.

"Taxi! Mass General, please!"

I could have taken the T. Not fast enough. The driver steps on the gas. The road is empty. Monday night. Still not enough.

"Sir, can you go faster?"

Eyes meet mine in the rearview mirror.

"It's an emergency!"

A nanoscopic moment. The back of his head is bald, badly combed over. The few remaining hairs are moon silver. Like the eyes and lashes. I don't know what he sees in the mirror and in the same nanoscopic moment, immense, but—

"You'll be there in four minutes."

We fly—he didn't lie—for four minutes.

Four minutes we spend in silence, I holding my breath, he the wheel. Four minutes is too short for talk; our lives just graze each other. He will not know what the emergency is. I will not know his name. How fragile, transient, shape-shifting, our little human existence.

Mass General. I burst out of the car, which drives on, to pick up another stranger. I run. Revolving doors whirl, propelled, like me, by something great and urgent.

Security. Elevators. Tenth floor. *Hurry.* No one in the hall. I tear past doors through which flash mothers, fathers, incubators, lives, other people's. Room 1013. Door open.

Naseem. Arrival, breathless arrival. My heart swells, soaked in warm honey.

It expands, overflows. Something pure, like an essence, flows out, through my pores, infusing the room with light. Transcendent and gold.

I have arrived. Naseem is asleep, dime-size chest rising, falling, barely, hovering like a feather on a breeze. The lights are off. I don't need them, not in here; I can deal with semi-dark now. A small blue vinyl couch against one of the walls. I curl into a ball.

November 2015

There were perhaps a hundred *douri* flitting delightedly around the slight woman in a coat with wide, stiff shoulders. Kays Deeb was not a large man, but his wife always seemed to float in his shirts and sweaters. Now, she almost disappeared in the brown folds of his coat.

Flashes of brown wings. Minuscule beaks unable to decide between happy squeaks and famished pecks at the crumbs she scattered. One bird deftly nipped a piece right out of her hand, causing Umm Hadi to squeak too. The coat flapped open.

A yellow dress with floral print. His mother owned four, all the same—local cotton, coarse but clean—in different colors: cream, pale blue, pale pink. She wore them in rotation. In summer, the fabric was too warm and scratchy. Now, in November, the crude stitching let in the icy breeze.

She clasped the coat shut with the hand that held the bag of scraps.

"There's a shortage of bread, you know." Hadi could not help the words, or their thin, short edges. There was a war going on. His mother did not respond. The flapping of wings was so loud he wondered if she'd heard. She broke off more crumbs.

"You're littering," he said, louder, unable to ignore the rising heat in his chest, and just below, the icy memory of hunger. It had not been long enough since Far' Falastin for him to forget. It would never be long enough. His mother was feeding the birds, while all across Syria, people were dying for bread. He had seen these people, had chanted with them in squares. In Far' Falastin, with those who got caught, like him, he had traded in bites of bread, smaller than those she was throwing away. One bite today was repaid as two tomorrow, if you survived till then.

His mother looked at him with big brown eyes.

"I'm not littering! Look, they're eating it!"

"They're eating our food!"

Her hand stopped midair. The sleeve fell back, and he saw a thin arm, freckles stark against the pale skin, that darkened, coarsened, chafed as it neared the red, swollen fingers. She put the last piece of bread back.

"It's stale," she murmured.

"I didn't think you'd want to eat it, Hadi," and he wished he had not spoken. He reached for her hand, idle now. Such a rare occurrence, she who—

"Mama, what happened to your ring?"

She slipped her hand in the coat pocket.

"Let's go home. I made mujaddara."

Lentils and bulgur, again. Then he noticed they hadn't had a single dish with meat since his release from prison. They had no milk or cheese either, but he had assumed the power cuts were the reason the fridge was empty and unplugged. He had gone off and gotten himself arrested, left his parents without money . . .

"Your baba will be hungry. We mustn't keep him waiting. He's tired."

She had sold her ring.

Baba was tired and hadn't pruned the trees or picked the fruits. They had lost an entire harvest. Mama kept her hand in her pocket. She held the bag and clutched her coat with the other. He put his arm around her small frame. He wanted to apologize. He squeezed her shoulders. Suddenly, she burst into sobs.

"I saw Omar's mother this morning, *miskina*."

"Still no news?"

She shook her head. Not since two nights ago. Three mornings ago, Omar had played offense, center right, and scored two goals with Zahi's football, in the lot behind the Douma municipality building, a stillborn construction site, now a graveyard for car shells and washing machines. When they were boys, Hadi and Omar used to play in the streets. The thrill, the risk, at any moment, of a car appearing, of being chased by a *shurti* . . . In Far' Falastin, they had told and retold each other the story of the one time they were chased, the grand epic of their escape, magnified, colored, with music. It had kept them laughing, and alive, busy constructing the caricature of the huffing, puffing, panting *shabiha* running after them.

"Mama, don't cry."

"His poor mother. *Haram, haram* . . . I keep picturing you . . ."

Omar fielding. Omar calling for the ball, shooting, running. Omar and Hadi running from tear gas in Marjeh. Omar whose sister Miriam had long black tresses and tasted of licorice when Hadi kissed her in the back seat of his friend's Renault.

No warning. They had just broken down the door of Omar's home.

Hadi gently began steering Mama toward the house. She stopped them abruptly, dropped the bag, her fingers gripping him as though she would never let go.

"I want you to leave Syria."

She said it in a whisper that seared them both.

"Mama."

"*Ismaa'ni*, Hadi. Go and don't you dare come back. There has to be a way. They're smuggling boys to Amman all the time."

"I can't leave you and Baba."

"*Habibi*, if they come for you next—"

"They won't! Listen to me." He tried to smile, but that only made her pound on his chest.

"You listen to me! I will not . . ."

She choked and lowered her voice and sobbed the rest into the crevice between them, where no ghosts or spies or passing neighbors could hear:

"I will not, I will *not* bury my son . . ."

The rest was drowned in the muted tears. Hadi held his mother closer. The top of her head did not reach his collarbone. She felt cold and paper-thin in his arms, which wrapped themselves too easily around her.

He held her until she was quiet and all else around them was too. Then he picked up the bag and they resumed their walk to the apartment.

"I made mujaddara," she said again. Tomorrow she would make fasoulia, Baba's favorite and his. They would never eat it; the *shabiha* would knock the pot to the ground. As for the mujaddara, they ate that in the basement, under a naked bulb.

Cluster bombs fell on Douma that night, and the temperature dropped. In the basement room, a neat stack of mattresses, a few cans of beans, coarse salt, a gallon of water, a propane burner, kerosene, and matches. Hadi counted twelve bombs. Baba, wrapping himself in his abaya, said no, no more than eight. The neighbors' children wailing. The neighbors themselves petrified into salt and stone, and in the midst of all that madness, Mama, in her nightshirt, began distributing plates.

Hadi's last dinner with his parents consisted of lentils, grains, and for dessert, a pack of dry cookies and a bag of sikkar nabat.

Precious, opalescent pebbles of hardened sugar. The biscuits would be stale in his memory, but the sikkar nabat would glisten like uncovered treasure. He would replay that scene a million times: Mama going around the circle, offering them, to the neighbors too, insisting everyone eat—only she had none—until the packet was empty. Mama proceeding to pick crumbs off the floor, put them in a bag. Tomorrow she would feed the birds. She found one piece of sugar, held it to the light to confirm. Iridescent. She ate it.

HADI

Six in the morning and there are already forty-nine or fifty shivering people ahead of me. Some look like they spent the night in front of the embassy. Within minutes, the queue snakes on behind me and wraps itself around the corner.

"*Yil'aan hal bard!*"

Curse this cold. The complaints are starting early.

The embassy gates won't open for two more hours. The first appointments are at eight. Everyone knows that. Everyone also knows never to come at eight. Even 7 a.m. is too late. Everyone knows there are caps. Well, except the visa virgins. Too bad for them.

They'll wait. They'll freeze out here. They won't get in. Tomorrow, they'll arrive sooner.

"*Wa yil'aan hal bahdaleh!*"

Curse this humiliation. Spittle hits the nape of my neck. I turn around: a meaty woman, sweat dribbling down her face, pooling under her armpits. She can't possibly be hot. No: Her lips are blue. Her teeth are chattering.

She's nervous.

Everyone else looks away. Everyone else is thinking, *You want to go to* Amrika? *Shut up and wait.*

Everyone else looks the same: an anxious, sighing group of eyes fixed on the gate, praying for it to open. Some are praying to the sky. Hands clutch the same manila folders containing the same precious documents. Nauseatingly hopeful.

"*Yil'aan hal bahdaleh.* These *Amrikan*, I heard they do it on purpose: make people wait, to discourage them from applying."

"*Yil'aanhon* and their visas!"

The man in front of me. A boy, I see as he fidgets. Early twenties. Trimmed beard. Gel in his hair. Black leather jacket as fake as his Armani watch. His cologne stinks. He should have shaved.

Americans don't like beards, and the guard, dark like the boy but clean-shaven, and with a gun, does not like his tone. His look shuts the boy up.

The kind of boy who gets shot down first in a demonstration. I was that kind of boy. He's sweating too. After him, no one complains. Instead, about an hour in, bored and cold, people start to make conversation. Transient, inconsequential, waiting-room conversation.

The perspiring woman declares, to no one and everyone, that she's going to visit her son, who goes to MIT. She says MIT twice, emphasizing the *I*, looks around. Silence. Disgruntled, she pulls something that smells sweet and looks sticky from a plastic bag. She shoves it in her mouth and swallows without chewing, then reaches into the bag for another.

An adolescent group of students—their tracksuits urge RUN FOR JORDAN!—eye her hungrily and chew gum. A wormy, worried young man goes through his documents. The third time he does, he drops them, yelps, scrambles to pick them up, and, almost in tears, puts them back in the manila folder, which he hugs. He asks a loud man in a loud three-piece suit—who could have been a pimp, but apparently, loudly, is a businessman—if he knows what time it is.

No mobile phones, no keys, no flash drives in the embassy. No sharp objects. The suited man looks at a gold watch. *Seven fifty-eight.* The conversations stop. Even the air seems to tense. Did I look like that years ago? Was I so dog-hungry?

I refuse to make eye contact with anyone. We're not the same, just in the same line. *I have a visa!* I want to say out loud. *I already live in* Amrika! I should be in another line. I want to go to the gate and tell the guards that I *had* a visa.

November 2015

There were about fifty people ahead of him in line. The smell of airport arrival halls was hypnotically foreign. Overhead, to entertain—or tantalize—the crowd, large screens played a muted video on loop:

Welcome to the United States of America!
We're so happy you're here!

The ethnic miscellany of travelers watched, transfixed, as the line crawled toward the understaffed passport control desks. Hadi was hypnotized too, drinking in, for the fourth time, the sunlit faces of every color, gender, age, and size greeting him.

In between those, variegated shots of the United States: cities, canyons, snowcapped mountains, apple orchards, cornfields. If his baba could see those . . . presidents' faces. Some he recognized, some not. Forests, interstate highways, horses galloping across vast . . . America the Great.

No bullet-ravaged buildings. No emaciated faces. A close-up of a hot dog in a baseball stadium. Baseball! Hot dogs! How he had fantasized about hot dogs on the harrowing journey to Amman from Douma. And donuts, and peanut-butter-and-jelly sandwiches, unable to even imagine such a concept. When they had crossed into Jordan and he had been allowed to stretch his legs at the Rukban settlement, a UN officer had actually given him one, with white bread!

Science fiction. The Boston Celtics, Thanksgiving, Saint Patrick's Day, hip-hop, rap, cheeseburgers . . . those things were real! And they were right outside, and he was almost there!

There was only one person left between him and the booth. A tall, lanky boy with long hair in dreadlocks and deep coffee-brown skin. He wheeled a carry-on and had a guitar case slung over his shoulder, completely covered with iron-on patches of—Hadi assumed—famous singers.

Hadi had a rucksack that contained a toothbrush, a half-empty tube of toothpaste, a half-used bar of olive soap with which he also washed his hair, wrapped in the newspaper he had taken from the embassy in Amman to practice his English.

The cookies had made a mess. At the airport, they had taken Baba's pocketknife and the bottle of water. And the four cans of tuna; no foreign meat allowed. No photos. They would have put his parents in danger if he'd been caught.

No flashlight. He had two sets of underwear and two pairs of socks. His khaki coat, he wore. He was, strangely, very cold. His teeth chattered, loud. The young man in front of him was in a hoodie and seemed quite comfortable.

Hadi put his hand in the inside pocket: ID, the lawyer's name and address and phone number. Other numbers: the embassy, his UN case officer, the house in Douma he had left. He knew that one by heart, but Mama had insisted, in a shaky hand.

She had also insisted, at the threshold of the door, her back straighter than he had ever seen it, on a white plastic bag she thrust into his hand, exuding fragrant thyme and sumac, containing three zaatar sandwiches.

The bread was already limp and heavy with olive oil. "For the road." The road to the United States of America. The sandwiches never left Douma: the oil seeped into the bag, he had to throw it out.

"I'll call you when I reach Amman."

"Don't you dare. They might be monitoring the phone. Don't call till you're in *Amrika*. On the *other* side."

He could see the other side, beyond the booth's plexiglass walls, clean and streak-free. He could also see his reflection, forehead and passport glossy. The latter he clutched fiercely, his hand slightly lifted, as though he were practicing presenting it.

Almost there! If he was in, if he was stamped in, if he just got past that booth . . . no more Molotov cocktails, locked doors, windowless rooms. No more Syria. He gripped his heart and took his bag, his sole companion, bruised and scratched from the journey. He would always be Hadi Deeb, son of Kays and Iman. He would bring them over, to this place where everyone smiled and there was so much space.

Land of Immigrants! flashed the words on the reel for the fifth time. A homeland for those without one. **Land of the Brave and Free!** The big block letters were almost bursting from the screen. Declaring that he, Hadi Deeb, could have all they were promising, if he was let in . . . One more stamp. The boy ahead of him was called. Behind him, people fidgeted.

HADI

At seven fifty-nine and fifty-nine seconds, the guard unlocks the gate. The queue advances, slowly, politely. Were this not the US Embassy, were the stakes not so high, had the guards not been wielding guns, the line would have, I'm sure, morphed into a rabid mob.

Each person is screened twice: once by hand, once by machine. The precious folders are opened, their contents scattered, glanced at, and left for their owners to gather; no one protests. They are nodded to, walk in, triumphant. None look back. Those outside look ahead, in silence. No more exchanges of quips and looks. Survival of the slyest.

Only two people remain ahead of me: the moody young man and a small woman I had not noticed before, who now takes a tube of lipstick from her purse—light pink, almost brand-new—and tries so clumsily to apply it to her lips that something in me catches.

Her red stubby fingers. Cuts and burns from chopping onions, stirring stews in pots. But her wrists are frail, sticking out of a padded coat. Which is black, not brown, so large the sleeves slide back to her elbows. The hopeless awkwardness with that lipstick she has never used before.

But it's the dress that grips me. The coarse cotton sleeve, blue flowers . . . She gives up on the lipstick and puts it back. She looks down. Her shoes are plain black, but polished, her hair undyed but clean and combed in thin, even lines.

She is called forward and gives the purse, worn but still decent, to the guard. With both hands. The gesture is painfully hopeful. He automatically empties the bag onto a tray, exposing its contents. It feels like some sort of violation. The lipstick breaks.

A pink mess. She jumps and her distress escapes her lips before she has time to catch it, and—

"*Yalla!* Let us in *ba'a*! I don't have all day!"

It happened so fast that by the time I turn my head toward him, the boy is already on the ground. Stupid, impatient boy, his nylon leather jacket torn. The woman is crying, also on the floor.

The contents of her purse are rolling out onto the street. He must have pushed her, trying to get past. The guard's black army boot is on his face, pressing it into the pavement. The boy's neck, exposed, like a bird's. It could snap like one. The M16 swings by the strap, midair, above him.

I knew that boy would be the first one shot in a demonstration. But this is not a demonstration. And this is Jordan, not Syria.

The guard merely yanks the boy up. Lucky *akhou sharmouta*. I think of Shadi, Ghaith, Omar . . .

"Go home! *Yalla!* Take your things and go home, now!"

"But I have an appointment!" the boy squeals.

How different from the fiery indignation of a few seconds ago. Young, so fucking young.

"You have nothing, *ya kalb*!" the guard howls. "Get out of here before I crush your face!"

They both know his boot could.

The boy yelps away like a wounded dog. When he is far enough, he shouts, "*Ayri feek!*" and runs.

The guard helps the shaking woman up. She made no sound since that shriek. My mother's breed of women cry silently. The handbag and folder are returned. She holds them to her chest the way a child hugs a stuffed animal.

"*Sitna*, what time is your appointment?"

"Eight o'clock," her small voice says.

"Do you have a printed confirmation?"

She nods and presents it. My heart chills. I don't.

"And your passport again, *sitna, law samahti*," the guard says politely, almost kindly to the lady. This man whose boot, minutes ago, almost crushed a boy's face. He runs his finger once, twice, three times down a three-page list. Meanwhile, the other guard looks over her shoulder at me.

"*Oustaz*, what time is your appointment?"

My eyes dash from boot to guns, to list, to gate. I lose my voice.

"*Oustaz*, your name and appointment confirmation, *law samaht*!"

"I . . . don't have one."

He raises an eyebrow. The two men exchange a bad, bad look.

"I mean, I already have a visa. I . . . I just need to ask a question. It's urgent. You see, it's about the travel ba—"

"*Sitna*," the first guard says, to the woman now, returning her documents, "your appointment was yesterday, not today. Go home and make another," as polite as he had been when he helped her up.

"But I was sure I—"

"I'm sorry, *sitna*. The embassy does not accept walk-ins."

"But I waited months for this appointment! Who knows when they'll give me another! My daughter is getting married, and we live so far from Amman . . . Please."

"I'm sorry, *sitna*," the guard says again and reaches over her shoulder to the next person. She bursts into tears. One yelp, then, a second later, she begins to gather her documents—passport, confirmation paper—on mute, shoulders shaking, sliding each item carefully back into the folder. She leaves. No one reacts, looking straight ahead at the land of their dreams.

"*Oustaz*, without an appointment . . ."

November 2015

It was the American Dream: the stand-alone house with the immaculate lawn. Green, because lawns were green here, because there was no shortage of water. He already knew there would be a barbecue in the back, and that in the spring, the bushes in front would bloom white flowers, and those in the pots under the windows, red.

They pulled up, and Mrs. Jeffries said, "Welcome home!" She had already become Corky, and Mr. Jeffries, "Paul, plain old Paul," before they had even left Arrivals. They had welcomed him with a placard and broad smiles, broad open faces flushed robust pink. His first view of America. They had driven across enormous, thickly forested land, on an enormous highway. More trees, more cars on more lanes, more space than he could even have dreamed. They had done all the talking, fortunately; he was too flabbergasted to speak. They worried, at first, that he couldn't understand them. "No, no." He just couldn't . . . believe.

A red, white, and blue flag hung over the garage door. He could almost see the bicycles that had lain strewn across the driveway when there had been children here.

There had been children. Two, "right about your age, son"—Mr. Jeffries had started calling him "son" before they had reached the car. Children who grew up in this house while he was growing up in Douma. Who belonged to this movie set of a world by birth; to this land, de facto.

"I hope you're hungry!"

Paul had taken his case, and Paul and Corky had taken him in. The Jeffries were Jewish. People in Syria would have been outraged. He would have been called a traitor. *Khayin.* But Syria was so far away. And Hadi was here, in this house in America, and would stay as long as he needed to find his feet on this land: a way to make a living, a place to live.

Paul would help him find a job. What had he done in Syria? In the spring, they could call some of the farms in Massachusetts. Meanwhile, there were heaps of restaurants all over Cambridge that always needed extra busboys, waiters . . . And, Corky said as she served him his first meal in America—enormous, like everything else: mashed potatoes, mac and cheese, brussels sprouts and meatloaf; when had he last had meat?—he could take night classes at the community college or the public library.

They gave him their son's old bedroom, for now. He met their son, their daughter, and her two dogs at Thanksgiving, when all came home. They insisted he keep the room; the kids were only there a few days. They had lives and homes elsewhere now. How normal, such a notion.

Everyone helped make the meal. There was a mess and much laughter and food disappearing. Everyone blamed the dogs.

The turkey took forever, was removed, undercooked, returned to the oven, and burnt. Corky served it proudly anyway. "Just add more gravy!" They did. Corky was a terrible cook. They smothered everything in gravy: the turkey, the potatoes, the brussels sprouts. Everyone raised a glass in her honor, and Paul kissed her on the lips. Hadi's parents would have been shocked. Suddenly, he missed his parents.

Everyone ate copious amounts of everything. Hadi had his first taste of cranberry sauce. It was so tart he spit some out in surprise. Cranberry on a white tablecloth! He looked at the stain, horrified, but Corky laughed.

"Darling, relax, it's just a tablecloth!"

Just a tablecloth. How easy it was to laugh; he had forgotten. How lightly, outspokenly, brazenly these people lived. How heavy Syria was.

After dinner, everyone cleared the dishes. Then came pie, coffee, more pie, followed by a migration to the sofas, where sated bodies stretched out. Hadi watched Paul and Corky doze off, holding hands, and his heart hurt for his parents. His baba and his trees, Mama and her birds. How far he was, that night, from them, in the stuffy rooms they had been born into and told were the world, papered with duty, sacrifice, windows and doors boarded.

Syria was not the world. He was sure of it now. Beyond it, there were lands where people kissed in public and ate turkey with jam.

Where people were Jews and Arabs but more, so much more than Jews or Arabs. Lands where people were just people, listening to Sinatra after dinner.

There he was, straddling both worlds on the sofa. That night he told Paul and Corky he wanted to bring his parents to America. As soon as he said it, the nebulous idea sprouted wings and turned into a plan.

He went to bed in a time capsule of someone else's life, one that could have been his: basketball trophies on a shelf; a shoebox filled, maybe, with squiggly drawings and sticky creations of bowtie pasta and string. In a drawer, candy wrappers and a stuffed rabbit with a frayed ear. Maybe his father could find work at one of those apple orchards. His mother could give piano lessons, make friends. He'd buy her a sturdy coat.

HADI

I'm here to see the consul! It's urgent."

I preempt the guard, and add, "I'm a refugee. I'm expected."

I don't know why I said that. Stupidity. Desperation. Too late now. I wait.

The embassy does not accept walk-ins. I can't be turned away. The woman who will likely miss her daughter's wedding disappears around the corner.

I look directly at the guard and wait for him to call my bluff. I wait for him to call the consul, or tell me there is no consul, or . . . He doesn't. I am screened, searched, motioned in. I stop a second, stunned, on the other side of the gate, then hurry up the path, not looking back, just like the others.

Waiting room.

"Take a number and a seat."

There are none that are empty. The room is bursting with anxious people clutching manila folders. I couldn't sit anyway. I just lied to a man with a gun. Ground under my feet. Sweat dribbling off my chin, down my neck and arms, darkening my shirt, to my wrists. Gelatin palms. I spot a water cooler and chug two cups in quick succession. The shock of ice to my insides. A faint scent of clean, lavender. Sharp inhale. Cough. Fucking lavender.

There is a window, closed, and all backs are turned to it. Everyone faces a row of counters crowned with little black squares. On those, red double digits ting, every once in a while, like slot machines. Every once in a while they make someone jump up like a lucky winner.

The summoned rush to the counters. Behind the glass windows, the officers barely look up. If they do, they look bored. They reach for documents through the opening, careful to touch paper, not skin, and follow procedure: File; fingerprint; ask questions; type; stamp—or not; slide paper back through the opening; then press a button. The double digits ting again. Someone jumps.

The system is perfectly oiled and perfectly aseptic. I am still coughing out lavender. I—and everyone else—wait.

What was that story about the man who died and found himself in a waiting room? He sat there for years, waiting for his judgment, until he couldn't bear it anymore. When he lost his mind, they said to him: "What did you think was going to come? You've been in hell all this time."

Ting.

Every head lifts, including mine. *Ting, ting,* over and over, until . . .

I jump up like a lucky winner.

*   *   *

"Passport and visa application," a faceless voice says.

"I'm not here for a visa. I'm here to see someone about the travel ba—"

"Passport and documents," the voice insists.

I fan my Syrian passport and documents on the counter, including Form I-275. A terrible hand. From the other side of the plexiglass, the officer looks at them. Then at me. He leaves the documents, untouched, between us, like a demarcation line.

"How can I help you, Mr. . . ."

"Deeb."

As it says on the first page of the untouched passport.

"It's about my refugee status. It was canceled this weekend after the travel ban."

"I see," the officer says in a tone that says he does not see at all. He picks up my documents now, reluctantly. Passport first. *Pass. Port. A pass across lands and seas into welcoming foreign ports.* He flips through it, silent as a wall. His fingers hover over the canceled travel permit, then change their mind. They pick up the last form, I-275, the one I signed.

"It says here you left the United States voluntarily," he says in a thinly veiled, but only thinly, accusing tone.

"No, I—"

" 'I understand . . .' " he starts to read the text.

"I know what it says, but it's not true! They made me sign it!"

He stops to look at me.

"They?"

Now he looks straight at me with cold, transparent irritation. In his eyes, I glimpse the sidewalk outside.

I blurt, all cards on the table: "Please, you must help me! My wife and child are alone in Boston . . ."

His look. He would have rolled his eyes at me were it not for *procedure*. Instead, he raises his hand as if to say *Enough*, as if to bolster the plexiglass border wall between us. He gathers my documents and slides them back through the slit—careful to touch paper, not skin—keeping Form I-275 and my passport. Then, wordlessly, he stands up and disappears with them.

I wait until, overhead, on the screens, the tings begin to appear in three digits.

A side door opens:

"Hadi Deeb?"

A stout woman with sensible shoes and a disapproving nose walks me down a corridor, up stairs, two flights, clacking through an antechamber in which a row of upholstered chairs line the wall. At their end, without a word, she leaves me at the door.

A woman at a cedarwood desk. Polished, both. She is young, conservatively dressed. Thick kohl. She does not look up from her screen. Her hair is an almost inky black. I remain at the threshold.

A blue Fatima hand on a gold chain on her neck. A strong smell of oud. An Arab woman's scent. A wealthy Arab woman's scent, but she is not—not even distantly—Arab. Iced coffee, brisk, efficient keystrokes. American.

An American abroad. An expatriate like me. Both of us displaced, groundless in this country. But no, she can always go home, whereas I . . . feel a sudden clenching in my stomach, on my tongue: a bitter taste.

I wait until she looks up.

"Can I help you?"

"I . . ." wish I'd worn a different shirt. I wish I had a different shirt. The smell of oud is overpowering. At least it will mask the sweat. I keep my arms glued to my torso.

"It's about my status."

"Are you a US citizen? For visa issues, you should make an appointment online—"

"Ma'am, they canceled my travel permit at Logan Airport over the weekend. They sent me back . . ."

I falter but watch her eyes cloud. She nods vaguely, says vaguely:

"The order . . . You must be—"

"Syrian, ma'am. I'm a refugee."

I launch into my story, like a race before I run out of breath or courage or her attention. I spill the words *Syria, order, a few days, parents, wife at the airport, NICU . . . They said I had to sign . . .* clumsy and discordant, like marbles from my pocket . . . *didn't have a choice . . .* the walnuts I stole from a street cart when I was five. I got caught then. A glided clock ticks behind her, quietly, like a bomb.

"Sir, let me stop you there."

Her eyes are the same opal blue as the Fatima's hand.

"If your permit has been canceled, there is nothing I or anyone here can do for you. We learned about Executive Order 13769 on Friday like everyone else."

It seems important that she use the full and exact title of the order, erecting it like the plexiglass wall of the officer. Protective, measures to distance her from feeling. Those must be job requirements.

"We are currently waiting to receive implementation guidelines. Until then, there is nothing—"

No! Wall or not, I bang against it:

"Ma'am, my wife and child are alone in Boston! My son is very sick."

And his name is Naseem, and mine is not 13769.

"Please! You have to help me."

Her eyes cloud again, and I know she sees me. She seems as lost as I am. Not all displacements are equal, yes, but she must recognize their scent.

"Please . . ."

She looks away, lifts a pen from her desk, and clicks it on, off, again. She chews on the end, looks to the door, at her screen, anywhere but at me. When she does, finally, the opal blue is thick, opaque.

"Look, you're the first person I've met who's actually affected by this. And I'm sorry, I really am. I . . . But there's a system in place for a reason, and there are people whose job is to issue guidance. Ours is implementation. We will follow the procedure once we know what it—"

"What does that mean?!" I burst. "What does all of that mean?"

No more heat now. The air cools.

"Sir, this is all the information I have."

"But what do I do?!"

"You have to wait . . ."

"Where? In Syria? You want me to get killed?"

"You could wait here—"

"How long? Jordanian visas for Syrians only last a month!"

"Then you have a month!" she shouts, and we both freeze.

Her powdered nostrils flare. She breathes in and tries again, measuring voice and tone:

"Sir, as I said before, I am sorry. We sent a dispatch to Washington over the weekend, expressing our concerns. This is difficult for everyone—"

"Everyone?!"

"Sir, we are all waiting . . ."

Powder and oud, and the gilded clock strikes ten.

Nothing has changed in the street. No cataclysmic debris. The sky is still icy, clear, just brighter. The queue still there, longer. They have their passports and I have been returned here with mine, my papers, my phone.

Not you, Samati. Not yet. I can't. Not at three a.m. in Boston. Another phone in Boston rings. Come on, pick up, Paul.

She said she was sorry, but *I have a meeting. Please leave your contact information with my assistant.* Paul, wake up. Answer the phone. She said we had to wait, but *Can you find your way out?* It was not she who had promised me America.

November 2015

Registry of Motor Vehicles. An oversaturated, windowless repository of waiting humans. A mishmash of buzzing, heavily breathing people, holding numbered tickets, thickening the air, drowning the ambient music.

He could hardly breathe, then someone closed the only door. Now Hadi couldn't breathe at all. Paul seized him by the arm.

"Let's take a walk."

Only outside the building did Hadi finally find air. He drew in greedy buckets while Paul watched and said nothing. They waited for the drumming in his chest to slow, slowly, infinitely slowly. Paul also seemed to hear it. When they both no longer could, the Syrian boy and his American lawyer looked across the street.

The trees in North End Parks were bare, except the conifers, which stood taller and insubordinately bluish green. Aleppo pines were a sandier green, and would now be shedding copiously, carpeting the red tile roof, spilling onto the windowsills, to Mama's dismay . . .

"You missed the foliage," Paul remarked quietly.

"If you'd come just a few weeks sooner, you would have seen colors like you can't imagine. Reds, oranges . . . Oh well, you'll see them next year. So, what was that about?" he said, like the thoughts were directly related.

Hadi himself couldn't explain what had just happened. The fear had not struck until after they had been asked to wait. Perhaps it was the government building, the uniforms, perhaps just the confined space. Perhaps, like his compulsion to crack open windows, leave doors ajar and lights on; like his inability to eat slowly, or stop till the plate was removed or his stomach screamed acid, some parts of Syria would always travel with him, no matter how far Syria was.

"I'm sorry, Paul. I don't know what got into me. I was just . . . suddenly I was . . ."

"Come on, son, you've got this! This is just the last step. Nothing to do but wait now. Once you get that state ID, it'll all be over. It'll be so liberating, and . . ."

That was the word: *liberating*. Freedom, so close at hand and so foreign, it terrified him even more than the RMV waiting room. He couldn't trust it. He didn't know how. The palpitations returned. He felt like a bird caught in a wind current. Paul had paused midsentence.

"You know what? Wait here."

He disappeared around the corner of Congress Street and returned, minutes later, with a paper bag. Pink and orange. In the other large, hearty hand, he balanced two medium coffees. He set his wares on the ledge under the Haymarket Station sign and pulled a thick, densely sugared donut from the bag.

"Eat," he said.

"I can't—"

But Paul shoved it in his hand.

"You look like hell. One bite. You'll feel better, believe me. This is all-American goodness."

Hadi took a bite.

"I put cream and two sugars in your coffee, like mine. I didn't know how you liked it, so I brought a few extra packets just in case you need them . . . Eat, son!"

Hadi took another bite. The donut was soft and warm, the sugar powdery. The coffee was good. He hadn't expected it to be.

"I went to school not far from here. When I was a kid, we used to run away, me and the boys, and hang out in that park there. We'd use our lunch money to get pizzas from Umberto's. Dang good slices. Nice and yeasty, with lots of cheese. Best pizza in the country."

He paused, then smiled.

"Actually, it was all we could afford, but it was good. Famous now. I heard they charge a dollar seventy for the slice. Scoundrels."

He outright laughed.

"We were such kids. Me, Billy, and whatshisname. Three skinny, funny-looking kids. Oh yeah, I was scrawny then"—loving nod to his belly. "We'd be at the door at ten forty-five, waiting for the place to open. We didn't know what to do with our freedom. Pizza in the park. Sometimes, after, we walked around. If one of us had extra money, we'd get cannoli. Have you had cannoli before? We'll get some later. For the life of me, I can't remember the other kid's name. Billy and . . ."

Omar. And all the other boys. And Hadi was here, and—

"It'll all be all right," Paul said, taking a bite and smiling with the white-dusted, blissful trust of a child. And in the very midst of a mad world, cut up so haphazardly into rooms with windowless walls and countries with sky and parks, Hadi ate every last crumb of his donut. And Paul had been right; it was goodness, all-American. He wiped his mouth.

"Thank you, Paul."

He waved his thanks away. Crumbs fell on his belly, which protruded in proud defiance of gravity. They sipped the last dregs of their coffee.

Paul said, "Son, I know it's hard, but you're going to have to learn to trust the system."

He threw the trash away. All that remained now was the ticket with their number from the RMV. Hadi would keep it. It would travel with him. Paul clapped him on the back.

"Now, we wait."

Approximately two weeks after a bird has felt the urge to leave—that "homesick," upward pull—it is overcome by a stronger lift. This feeling seems to affect the members of an entire flock synchronously. It flies off in one sweeping, perfectly choreographed movement.

This unrehearsed synchronicity—the ability of thousands of birds in a single flock to suddenly take off, flying in such dense swarms without colliding—continues to baffle ethologists. It can only be assumed that this behavior is driven by evolutionarily developed instincts.

Zugunruhe describes the angst birds seem to feel when seasons change and the migration period begins. Even a caged bird "knows" it should be traveling too. They hop about, flutter their wings, and flit from perch to perch.

February 3, 2017

SAMA

The knock at the door jolts me upright.

"So this is where you've been."

Through the fog between sleep and wake, at the door, a vague figure in tweed. I know that voice.

"Sir?"

The phone slips from my hand to the floor. Diving to pick it up, I follow. Rising, I ram my head on the bottom of the couch. Professor Mendelssohn looks elsewhere with his round glasses.

"For a while, I thought you may have taken off to South America. You know, followed your red knots, for research. Why else would you have missed our meeting *and* not even sent those chapter edits?"

His mustache is combed, each hair straight and pristine. He looks as serene as I feel ravaged by the past few days. My clothes are coffee-stained and I must have couch prints on my cheek. I push away damp, tangled strands of hair plastered to my face. The motion revives a soreness that keeps deepening every day.

The couch is hard to sleep on; the air-conditioned room, glacial; the lights, the beeps punishing, but there is no world for me beyond this room. And yet, at its door . . .

"What are you doing here?"

He sidesteps the question and enters the room. His gaze is clear and placid, as though his appearance on the NICU floor at Mass General Hospital, on a Friday morning, were the most natural occurrence. I realize I have never seen him outside campus. Under the harsh spotlights, without a desk between us, he looks whiter, more silvery, smaller. Still, he smiles, and I instantly feel like a lost child who got found.

"I took the liberty of printing out my comments on the last pages you sent."

"How did you—"

Wry smile.

"There are only so many places a pregnant woman can disappear to. Everyone on the faculty sends their best. Also, I borrowed a few books from the library I suspect you already know, but that I thought would be good company."

He waves a brown paper bag I only just noticed.

I want to speak but my throat is sealed shut. I want to take his hand. Instead, I fumble with my sweater and try to smooth my cheek and forehead. He turns away discreetly and sets the bag beside the incubator.

"Why, hello, little friend."

Smiling at him, he asks, "How is he?"

Still struggling to breathe. Heart rate erratic. Weak. Blood pressure low . . . but gaining weight, and no complications last night . . . and it is so good to see Mendelssohn. I open my mouth and croak. He turns to me. Gold-rimmed eyes. Water blue. Baba's are brown. The thought appears, lightly, from nowhere.

"And how are you?"

Just as lightly, the question shatters me like a crystal vessel.

I burst into tears in a very cold, windowless place. Professor Mendelssohn does not say anything. He waits.

When I pause for air, he pulls a cotton handkerchief from his breast pocket. I used to think no one in the world but Baba still used those. The sight of that little square of cotton, thousands of miles from home . . . I could have cried into his shirt. I could have cried myself to Damascus. Instead, I cry into the cotton, and he waits for me to finish.

He does not speak immediately into the silence that follows. He lets it settle. Machines beep, and I am grateful. I return the hand kerchief, soggy. He folds it delicately then, with clear eyes, says, "Do you like poppy seeds?"

First, I think I misheard, then that I misunderstood. Then, while I am still deciding, he says:

"My wife sent you flódni. It's a traditional Hungarian cake with apple, walnuts, poppy seeds, and jam. Hers is quite good. I left it at the nurses' station."

He continues: "Also, she wants to know if you like chicken paprikash."

"I, I've never had it," I stammer.

"It's not too spicy. Just paprika and some pepper, I think. You will try it next time. Meanwhile . . ."

He reaches for the paper bag and pulls them out, one by one, old friends: *The Land's End, Birds and Green Places . . .* W. H. Hudson. The room blurs again and I blubber:

"Sir, I—"

"Just so you don't stray too far," he says without looking at me and opens one at random. Midnight-blue cover.

" 'It has been observed that birds feel a sort of pain before taking off. A pain, almost like fear . . .' Perhaps fear," he remarks to himself. " 'Nothing alleviates that feeling except the rapid motion of wings.' "

He shuts the book and says, without checking his wristwatch, that he has a class to teach. The others will be dropping in and out, with lasagnas, pies, casseroles. If I need more books, I should just ask.

"Sir, I—"

But he waves it off and leaves me in a room that suddenly feels less cold.

At the threshold, he picks up an envelope someone must have slipped under the door.

November 2016

There was food, more than twenty people could or should ever eat. Food as any gathering of expatriates mandated. Arab expatriates, said the gold and lapis knickknacks, the Persian carpets, and etched mirrors that cluttered Al Firdaos Middle Eastern restaurant.

The place was embalmed with rose incense, to mask the garlic perhaps. Loud oriental music competed with loud voices: Arabic in an array of dialects, English in accents betraying varying stages of expatriation. All buoyantly, boisterously celebratory: *"Mabrouk!"* Toasting Sama's pregnancy.

Shots of milky arak and glasses brimming with Tyrian wine. Trays of kibbeh and sambousek, tabbouleh, mashawi. Hummus and labneh and soft pockets of bread, still puffed with steam. Overhead, through the speakers, Fairuz sang melancholically.

Sama hated Fairuz and such gatherings. She hated the singer's drawling voice and never-ending list of longings. Hadi listened to Fairuz as he shaved every morning.

Hadi loved Fairuz, as his father did, and Sama's father, and, she suspected, most of the people at this table: Hadi's friends, whom he'd made at the Lebanese sandwich shop where he worked, six days a week, long hours for minimum wage, sometimes on Sundays too, for, as the owner explained, "there are no Sundays for us hardworking immigrants."

Us. The owner was a portly Syrian businessman who ran a shabby establishment in an as-yet-ungentrified neighborhood in Cambridge. A warmhearted countryman who had kindly offered Hadi a place behind the counter, forty-five minutes and two bus rides away from their apartment.

Sama wanted Hadi to take classes, perhaps get a degree, play the piano again, meet her Harvard friends. Americans. He would, when he was ready, he said. He wasn't then. He liked the sandwich shop. He felt at home on that street of ethnic, eclectic small businesses that sold nail care, food, car repair, religion . . . all the same thing, really: a sense of community. A construct, like any, that the lonely create to make themselves feel less lonely.

His clientele flocked in, ravenous, almost all immigrants, almost all blue-collar workers, shelling out their precious dollars for street food that cost five times more than in Damascus. Homesick and hungry, proportionally. The sandwiches were mediocre, but the place was always packed, especially at that hour, blue, near the end of the day when everyone else seems to have somewhere to go, to be. Sundays, especially . . . At such times, it was nice to step out of the street and into a place that smelled of bread and thyme, even for five dollars, if only for five minutes.

Hadi reached for another *man'ousheh*. It tasted like shit. But also like Syrian mornings, the zaatar flatbread baked to just golden in Abu Riad's *furn* on the way to school: folded, bubbly, and still steaming, into a crescent. The scent of sumac and thyme would trail down the street behind him. If he closed his eyes, he could just feel the warm, puffy dough dissolve on his tongue.

Sama was not eating. There was too much food. They always ordered too much food. And the camaraderie, the music, were too loud. And the makeup on the women. They wore thick kohl and painted their lips so red that every glass but Sama's was stained with prints like red cherries. She felt consciously pregnant.

It was so situational, time-bound and shallow, this affinity they shared. They teased her about her accent and when she forgot certain words in Arabic. They inquired about Haa'vad. She had avoided such gatherings for years, and only been to that fundraiser for refugees last year out of some sense of duty to . . .

Hadi turned to kiss her, eyes bright. He whispered in her ear, his breath licorice-sweet with arak: "Are you having a good time?"

She had met him at that fundraiser. She had married him. And this loud and motley crew of Arabs was well-meaning and generous. And in the absence of a baba, mama, or any family in the US, they were offering food and warmth and it felt safe.

"I know you don't really like hanging out with the expats, but I thought it would be nice to celebrate . . ." Hadi began, anxious at her silence.

"I'm having a lovely time," Sama said and smiled broadly and meant it.

Lebanese wine and conversation flowed. Opinions rose and ebbed.

"Have you chosen a name yet? If it's a boy, Kays, like Hadi's father?" asked one of the girls, long black hair, long nails, long lashes.

"Why the hell would they do that?" said another, whose hair was cropped short, blue black reflecting large gold hoops that hung from delicate ears.

"People here will just mispronounce it and the kids at school will tease him! Sama, pick an American name. Something really American. Brian."

"Brian?! What will people say when they go to Syria?"

The man sitting across from Hadi grumbled, "Syria? Who's going to Syria? Fucking shelled-out country . . ."

"Watch your mouth, Salim!"

They couldn't have looked more similar, the two dark-haired, dark-bearded men; they even both came from Al Ghouta. But Salim had left with his mother and father after the chemical attack in August 2013. Someone said he maybe had a baby sister who died, but all he ever said was that "they fucking ruined the summer." He spoke with no accent.

Ahmad, across from him, manned the shawarma wheel at the sandwich shop where Hadi worked. He and his wife always smelled faintly of garlic and onions, and they had won the green-card lottery years ago. Sama always wondered why they had entered it.

Ahmad pounded the table. "Our fathers, our brothers, are fighting for that shelled-out country of yours, Salim! You're eating that shelled-out country's food!"

"Exactly, Ahmad! I'm eating it *here*! I'm eating falafel in America, where I'm safe, and so are you, by the way."

"You think you're safe here? Have you seen the news? Did you see who the Americans just elected?"

"It's a free country!"

"Not for us, my friend! It's not *our* country!"

They didn't come from the same Syria, the exile and the patriot-from-a-distance.

"Oh, *come on*, Ahmad! Don't be a hypocrite! You've been in America how long now?"

"That's not the point! Unlike you, I haven't forgotten my *ousoul*!"

"Ah, your *ousoul*!"

Salim laughed.

"Tell me, Ahmad, what is your *ousoul*? Your mother's food? Your father's olive trees?"

"Our heritage! Our land!"

"Oh, *yil'aan abouk*, go back to it then!"

Both men had risen, with their voices, from their seats. Both realized it and sat down. Ahmad's wife passed him a piece of cheese wrapped in fried phyllo dough. He bit into it. Chewy: It had gone cold. He finished it and took another. Salim downed the rest of his cloudy white arak and reached for the carafe. He poured himself another generous, licoricey shot.

"Go back to Syria then, Ahmad," he said, coldly, again.

"Tell me how you like it, whatever it is that's still there . . ."

"Our people," Hadi interjected. "Our people are still there." He said it quietly, his hand clutching Sama's under the table, her ring cool and soothing under his skin. He hadn't given her a proper wedding: the party, the dress, the hired *zaffeh* hoisting her on their shoulders over family and friends. These people, this dinner, so rapidly turning sour, this was the best he could manage.

He looked down. He hadn't even been able to give her his mother's ring. His mother's white, bare fingers, the wrist bone on her bare hand. He hadn't been able to give his mother and father reunification visas. Yet.

"What people, Hadi? You're not one of them anymore."

Salim responded quietly too.

"You'll always be the man who left, even if you do return."

A rare and sad, foreign silence followed. Coffee arrived, just then, on a silver platter, with plates of sesame barazek and knafeh doused in thick syrup. People looked down at their plates. Some did not touch them; some wiped them clean. People fill voids differently. Salim drank two scalding shots of coal-black Turkish coffee, then said, hoarse, his throat burnt:

"Look, we all left. Let's stop kidding ourselves." He wore a Red Sox jersey. "You live here now, Hadi."

"And I'll always be a foreigner here."

Salim shrugged. "With clean water to drink, a roof over your head, and one day, maybe, a nice backyard with a swing set for that kid . . ."

He smiled at Sama, but she was looking at Hadi, who seemed like a child trying hard to find a word. Finally, he said, "My kid won't know Syria."

Salim was gentle, but merciless: "Or the difference between an M-21 and a 120-millimeter mortar."

SAMA

The envelope is addressed to Mr. Naseem Deeb, in a cursive font printed in deep, royal-blue ink. My thumb traces every letter, to be sure it is there, then I turn the envelope over and break the seal.

The Commonwealth of Massachusetts
United States of America
Certificate of Birth

The words sound warm in my head; they trickle like honey. The paper is thick and luxuriously heavy. Its weight on my palm is sober and safe. This is not a dream. I press the document against the incubator's transparent wall.

"Look, little one. Look . . ."

Naseem is drifting in his world, untouched and unmarked by ours.

"That's your name, *ya zghir.*"

This is your ticket. Out of that box, this room, to a world different, so different from mine. It's magnificent. I see it.

You'll say your first words in English, take your first steps on grass, know the smell of earth after September rain. You will know snow, build snowmen. You will know how to throw a baseball, and Teta's lullabies, and the taste of peanut butter, sumac, thyme, toasted pine nuts.

Your sun will rise over an ocean. Mine rose, for the longest time, over arid mountains. Naseem, your sun will rise over liquid horizons. Those will be wider and farther than even I could ever dream. You'll have origins, not roots. You'll have wings. Wait till you see the sky, Naseem.

Wait till you look out the window. The earth is pink and yellow. The morning sun has colored the Charles River purple. The air itself is chiffon layers of lavender. There is so much of it, so much space. It is a very beautiful world.

Wait till you see it. Wait till we tell your father . . .

February 3, 2017

SUSPENSION OF EXECUTIVE ORDER 13769
Federal Judge Temporarily Halts Travel Ban

A US District Court Judge has temporarily blocked the key provisions of the January 27, 2017, travel ban nationwide. US Customs and Border Protection informed major American airlines that it was "back to business as usual," and the State Department has reversed the cancellation of visas—so long as those visas were not stamped or marked as canceled. It is estimated that 60,000 already were.[1]

HADI

You have reached Jeffries and Associates, attorneys at law. We're sorry we missed your call. Please . . ."

I need to punch something. The TV screen, the wall. The window, if it will break. I need something to break. My fist has to bleed. Some bone in it has to crack. I need to hear it. I need to hear my howls echoed back to me by the walls, these fucking walls. *El a'ama!* I need to stop howling, stop shaking.

"You have reached Jeffries and Associates, attorneys at law. We're sorry we missed your call. Please . . ."

Please pick up! Pick up, Paul! My thoughts thrash around the room like a goldfish mad in its bowl. Dusty rays of sun through the glass, and a fly. And I . . . The screen on the phone turns dark. No answer. *Paul!*

I cannot unclench the phone. In my other hand: my passport, mucking, fucking passport. *That* I can throw. I hurl it at the TV, but it just falls, pages fluttering, to the ground. Pathetic, and the news has moved on now to other things, the weather, done with the travel ban, done with me.

"Fuck! Fuuuuck! *Yil'aankon!*"

Yil'aan who? Fuck who? There is no one here but me, and my passport. Pass-fucking-port. Which port? Which country will take me now?

"I was in!"

I scream at the muted screen, cough, retch, choke on saliva, snot, and tears. *I had a fucking visa! You took it away from me! I groveled like a dog for that visa!*

The room swirls. I grip the phone.

"You have reached . . ."

"Hello?"

"Paul! The news . . . The judge . . ." I croak, lungs raw, throat burning.

"I'm so sorry, Hadi," and I know it's over. "The ruling is clear: If the visa was already canceled—"

"No!"

It blasts out of my chest.

"Don't tell me you're sorry, Paul! Tell me what we're going to do now!"

"Hadi, at this point, there's really—"

"I could return to the embassy. You could call the State Department . . ."

"They can't help, Hadi."

"Well, who can, Paul?!"

Silence. As he breathes, the walls around me appear to crumple, shrink, as if the air were being sucked out of the room, as if air were escaping through the receiver, swelling the space between Boston and Amman.

His voice comes from far away:

"Maybe, in time . . ."

"What time, Paul? I have no time! My Jordanian visa expires in a couple of weeks. Then what do I do? Where do I go?"

My own voice races desperately out of the room, through the phone.

"I have a wife and son waiting for me! I need to go home!"

November 2016

He slipped the coat around her shoulders and helped her zip it up. Nearly midway through her pregnancy, she was just starting to round. He had bought her that coat, a serious, no-joking-about-Boston-cold coat, with his own first, proud paycheck. Hadi Deeb, employed.

It was white and had been delivered in a large white box tied with a velvet bow, the color of deep midnight. She had kept the ribbon, because she did such things, his wife.

"*My wife,*" he had said, over and over at that dinner with the expats, amazed each time he heard it. Amazed whenever he could hear it: it had been one loud, raucous dinner.

It had felt almost like home. He had spoken in Arabic, loud, and been understood, and had laughed and eaten and drunk. But toward the end, the arak had run out. The food and talk of Syria had begun to weigh heavy in his stomach.

And now, most of the chairs were empty, and outside, it was dark.

The door opened and shut. Cold air blew in, and he caught a sudden whiff of that blue Sunday smell that hung about the patrons of the Lebanese sandwich shop. It seeped, swift and damp, into his open coat. He felt keenly adrift, lost.

Never had he been so far, felt so far away from all he knew to be familiar. Even in this restaurant, where, minutes ago, he had been surrounded by his compatriots. Salim was right; he didn't belong in Damascus anymore. But Hadi knew he didn't belong in Boston either. He was in-between, somewhere, nowhere, suspended over the Atlantic, speaking in English and singing Fairuz in Arabic. Free to go where and be who he wanted, as unbound as he had ever been, and as uprooted. His fingers were clumsy, but he finally pulled up the zipper.

"Thank you, *hayati*."

She touched his arm and he felt a sudden rush of safety, hot and concrete. He put his hand over hers, to keep it there.

"I look like a giant marshmallow," she grumbled.

She did not. She looked small, vulnerable, flushed. Pregnant with his child. Once more, he wondered why and how he, Hadi Deeb, had come to be holding her arm, in Boston, in a Middle Eastern restaurant. Sama Zayat wavered but he held on, to her and the confluence of their lives, just then, like a lifeline.

In the street, they were both briefly stilled by the quiet openness; it had been loud in there. A mildness unimaginable for a Boston November. They walked at her pace.

"Did you have a good time?" he asked.

"I did. Thank you so much for the surprise. I hadn't had a man'ousheh in years! I didn't even know I missed it."

"Really?"

She stopped them both to stand on tiptoe and kiss him on the lips. Then they walked, and he was silent.

"What about you? Did you have a good time? . . . Hadi?"

"It was fine."

The words came out gruffer than he had intended. He had been drifting away again. They reached an intersection and he realized they should have turned sooner. He didn't recognize the white facades, the dark violet windows. They were lost, they realized, and Sama groaned: "I really need to use the bathroom."

"Again?"

Pregnancy bladder. Panic. Cab. Mad race through the streaking red, yellow, green traffic lights, past white lampposts and the orange windows of living rooms, the moonlit river, Cambridge . . .

Finally! *Hadi Deeb, Sama Zayat,* next to the blue front door. She fumbled for the keys she had already given him. Quick! They'd check the mailbox tomorrow. He waited while she gathered breath and courage: four flights of steps.

"Soon I'll be too pregnant for this! You may have to carry me."

She puffed and tried to smile and tripped.

"I might have to start carrying you now!"

They reached the top floor and she flew into the bathroom. A few minutes later, coming out, she said, "I don't know what I'm going to do when the kicking really begins."

Hadi smiled. "Bladder football," he said, then thought of something. "Americans call it soccer."

"So?"

He was silent. It returned, that unmoored feeling from the restaurant: their child would be American.

"Hadi, are you all right?"

"Our child won't speak a word of Arabic," he blurted.

For a moment, she just looked at him, then took his hand. They went to the couch. On the coffee table lay the Lonely Planet guide to Syria. In it, the food and songs and vistas of orchards and Sundays and he and the boys kicking Zahi's football in the municipal lot. None of it would mean anything.

"Maybe," Sama said, "maybe not. Maybe our child will speak five different languages, be a poet . . ."

"It doesn't bother you?"

She thought about this for a while.

"I chose to leave Syria—"

"You were forced to. We all were."

She shook her head.

"I made a choice, and I chose to come here. I could have gone anywhere. I chose this country . . . Hadi, what is the difference between an M-21 and a 120-millimeter . . . ?"

Mortar. The first was a rocket. One learned to hear the difference after enough hours spent hiding in the basement. Hadi looked at Sama and at where he was, on an Amazon-green sofa.

"It doesn't matter," he said. He was no longer lost. His wife and child didn't need to know the difference between a mortar and a rocket.

He sat with his wife on the sofa, breathing the scent of red apples and vanilla in her hair, listening to the last notes of the lingering Fairuz song in his head. The *lahn* . . . the melody returning to its original cadence. He said, "You know, I think you're right: Maybe we should get a piano."

HADI

Hadi? *Habibi?*"

I shouldn't have called. In the background, someone shouts:

"*Khalti!* The onions are burning!"

I can hear and smell the sizzle.

"*Harkihon!* Turn the fire down and stir. Sorry, Hadi, *habibi*. The neighbors are here, the Haffars, and Umm Omar and Miriam. Bless them, they brought lamb."

Falling off the bone, silken, into its own juices. Toasted pine nuts. Rice, fluffy, steaming, with gold sha'iriyeh.

"Hadi, *habibi. Ya 'omri . . . keifak?*"

I am . . . suddenly starved, for that micro world I can hear in the background. Voices, bits of meat and onion sputtering in a pot. The price of leaving it resounds through the phone, in my ears, my stomach. Hollow.

Clanking plates being set on a kitchen table dressed with a plastic cover and a glass bowl of green olives. Baba's olives, in the olive oil he pressed—how many jars does Mama have left? Mama, in an apron, wiping a wet brow with a kitchen towel.

"*Keifik inti*, Mama?"

In Baba's brown coat, shivering in the morgue. Mama without Baba, smaller than I remembered, shoulders hunched, a widow waving like a child from the window of the bus that took her back to Douma without visa, husband, son.

"How are you? How is the *wad'* outside?"

The "situation," that eerie euphemism for the clashes, arrests, abductions, shortages, torture and death rates.

"The *wad'* is the same," she says. "People keep visiting. Umm Omar comes every day"—a grieving mother comforting a widow—"and did you know, Miriam is pregnant?"

Miriam's long licorice hair falls like a veil in front of my eyes. "Inshallah, a boy this time!" I hear Umm Omar say. Inshallah, Umm Omar . . .

"*Mabrouk*, but, Mama, how are you? Do you have water, electricity? Is someone bringing you—"

"They cut the water all over the city. You should see the lines at the wells. People freezing for hours, but the Haffars' boy has been filling plastic bottles for me every couple of days. And Abu Riad brings bread. Everyone has been kind."

She is silent a moment.

"Can you talk in the living room, Mama?"

Slippered footsteps.

"It looks like there are ghosts in here. I covered the furniture, except for the piano."

"Why, Mama?"

"The house is too big, *habibi*. I'm alone. I don't need such a large room, and the kitchen is easier to heat. I may sell the house. The orchard—"

"I'm sorry, Mama."

For a moment, in Amman, she was the child and I took care of her, of the ugly papers that clung like leeches to Baba's death. I tried to salvage her visa appointment. I took her to dinner at the nicest restaurant I could find. She tried to pay, then said she didn't want coffee and was too full for crème brûlée. I ordered two of each, and the next day pulled all the cash I could from the ATM. I waved and promised at the bus pulling out of the station, in diesel fumes and mist, but now . . .

"*Ya habibi, ya* Hadi, don't cry . . ."

"Mama, I'm so sorry . . . Don't sell anything! I'll send you money. I . . ."

Can't lie anymore.

"I can't go back to the US, Mama. My status is revoked for good."

Mama is silent.

"I can't get you a visa. I'm sorry. I'm so sorry. It was all for nothing . . ."

Years and forms and DNA tests and medical exams, paperwork and fees and the promise of "family reunification," and Mama and Baba all the way to Amman, so he could die, waiting, and she . . .

"It's all right, *habibi*. Shh, it's all right, *ya zghir*."

"I'll come back! Don't sell the orchard! I'll—"

Care for the four plum trees, the apple tree.

"Don't you dare! *Istarji*, Hadi! *Majnoun?* They'll kill you!"

Her voice drops to a whisper.

"You want to be a martyr, like Omar? That will kill me, *habibi*. I can't . . ." She breaks off. "*Baa'dein*, your place is with your wife and child. You will find a way back."

"Mama, I—"

"Find a way back to them, Hadi."

She is silent in her darkened, cobwebbed room.

"I'm tired, Hadi."

"*Khalti!* Come eat!" Miriam calls from another room, one where I once had a seat at the table. In this disintegrating world, there is a kitchen with towels on which my mother painted birds . . .

"I'll send money," I say.

"Don't worry about me, *habibi*. I don't need anything. *Noshkor allah*, I have a roof over my head, food . . ."

Lamb and rice she will barely touch, and yesterday's bread, which, when everyone goes, she will eat, hard, sprinkled with salt. She will save the crumbs to scatter under the terebinth tree for the birds, if there are any in February. If not, the crumbs will wait for spring.

"Don't worry about me, *habibi*," she says softly, small and fragile as the *douri* she loves.

"*Yalla, khalti!*"

And Mama hangs up.

Scientific research has indicated that long-distance migrants play a crucial role in shaping and preserving ecosystems around the world. They prey on pests, pollinate flowers, carry seeds across seas and continents.

Seventy percent of New Zealand's forests come from seeds dispersed by birds. The Micronesian imperial pigeon alone disperses seeds across the entire Palau archipelago, over 550 islands. And with the billions of birds that fly from Europe to sub-Saharan Africa every year, millions of seeds travel too. Researchers believe this function could save many species in the face of climate change.

Migrant mortality, however, has increased significantly in recent years, due to predation, hunting, and habitat loss at stopover sites. The latest research has found that a third of the billions of birds who migrate annually no longer return.

February 11, 2017

FEDERAL AGENTS CONDUCT
IMMIGRATION ENFORCEMENT RAIDS

Hundreds of undocumented immigrants have been arrested in at least half a dozen states this week, as US immigration officials move swiftly to enforce the travel ban, with states like Florida, Kansas, and Texas, and Northern Virginia witnessing a particularly high number of raids . . .

Beyond being in violation of immigration law, the individuals detained and deported seemed to possess no criminal record.

The arrests sent waves of shock and fear through all immigrant communities across the country, raising concerns of legal immigrants being targeted next[2] . . .

SAMA

On television, muted scenes alternate. Men, mostly young, most Latino, handcuffed and shoved into vans, under the chilled orange and blue of LA streetlights and flashing sirens. Crowds blocking intersections, waving arms, crying, shouting, in silence too. No point in turning the volume on; the commentary will be as grainy as the videos, as confused, also looping. And nasal. A voice that would clearly prefer to be reporting the latest sex scandal.

That follows, swiftly. The news and America move on to the next story. Then entertainment, sports and the weather, stocks. I keep the TV on, still.

"Sama, are you still watching?"

Your voice sifts through the phone, thick, murky, muffled, almost forcefully calm.

"I can't stop crying."

"Where will they go?"

"Sama! Turn the TV off!"

The newscaster is back, mouthing in silence, her lips plump, rosy, shimmery. Her eyes glaze, moving left to right, over words on the teleprompter. Then the boys again. I see us. Give me your tired, your poor . . . Everyone wants America.

"I called Paul. He says they're not going after people with visas yet, just the undocumented. As long as the travel ban is still on hold, you should be safe . . ."

US PRESIDENT PROMISES NEW TRAVEL BAN
"TO PROTECT OUR PEOPLE"

In response to the federal court decision pausing his travel ban, the president has vowed to issue a new immigration executive order within a week.

SAMA

Everyone wants America because everything is better here. Everyone always has, and before America, somewhere else, because everything is always better elsewhere. That's why people crouch, freezing in meat trucks, cram onto rubber dinghies they know may capsize in the middle of the ocean. That's why we came, isn't it?

Give me your tired, your poor . . . Everyone wants America.

"Hadi, what do we do?"

Hadi, it's been weeks since I saw you. Hadi, time has stopped and we have stopped, you and I, on either side of a moving world.

"Hadi, are you there?"

Your voice seems to come from farther and farther away each day, and each day, I discover a silence on these calls of a different color, falling like a shade, thickening this distance. It's blocking the sun and—

"Hadi!"

"Give me a fucking moment to think, Sama!"

—sucking the air from my lungs.

Finally, words, forced and quiet, like they just passed through cement:

"I'd hoped the illegal immigrants would keep them busy . . ."

You stop.

"I didn't mean it like that."

"I know," I lie too. We sit in the silence that can only follow such a statement, thundering with the proof of what this nightmare has made us.

Us. And *them.* When did we become that? We're all tired and poor, we're all exiles in some way: immigrants, refugees. There is always a reason people leave. Life, liberty . . . Everyone wants America, but not everyone is equal. And the truth, the traumatizing truth, is that if you and I had US passports, or green cards, if we had come to this country sooner, been the ones on the inside . . .

"*Yil'aanhon.*"

"What did you say?"

Behind the cement wall, you whisper:

"Fuck them, all of them. Fuck Jeffries."

"Hadi! He's trying to help us—"

"Sama! They don't want us there! We're all the same to them, foreigners, aliens! They don't want us! Fuck them! Fuck the embassy, the consul—"

"What consul?"

You burst into laughter.

"You're right. Maybe it wasn't the consul I met at the embassy. Maybe it was the First Lady herself! What an honor . . . there was nothing she could do, of course. Nothing anyone can do. She was very, very sorry, then she threw me out like a dog! Fuck her, and fuck Jeffries!"

"Hadi!"

"Fuck them all!"

An explosion of coarse, gasping, rasping coughs. A terrifying silence follows. Not thunder now; like going deaf. Tar, the color of this silence.

"You have Naseem's birth certificate?"

"What?"

"Answer me!"

"Yes."

"Okay. Find out what you have to do to get him a passport. Pack up the apartment, sell whatever you can, take all the cash, empty our accounts . . ."

Slowly, horrifyingly, I start to understand.

HADI

A sudden fist of coarse, dry sand hits me in the face; khamsin, the storm that haunted my childhood every year. Fifty days, khamsin.

It gusts into the hotel room through the crack in the window I made, covering, in an instant, every surface with red dust. *Yil'aanak. Yil'aankon. Fuck you all.* I slam the window shut. Instantly, Room 204 and all of Amman become a prison again. Sand grates my lungs.

Minibar bare. The wind outside howls. Red, swirling sand. I wait. I hear Baba's voice from a vanished time and place say, "Just fifty days."

I was five and I believed him. It was all I could do. And all we could do was wait, fifty days indoors—we couldn't breathe— while the winds whizzed and wreaked havoc like missiles, ruining crops, uprooting trees, cloaking Douma in darkness the color of dry blood. And Baba at the window, looking out, repeating *just fifty days*, while his orchard was decimated.

Baba, Douma seem so far away. Time is a terrible distance. You seem so far away, Sama. I'm waiting on the phone. The seconds, treacherous, engorge the chasm between Amman and Boston. I cannot hear your thoughts, picture the look on your face. I can't even see out the window. Only a streetlight, hazy. A spot of mustard amid the copper dust, against the glass, like a stain.

I wait for the storm, inevitable.

"You want Naseem and me . . . to come to Amman?"

I expected you to shout. You do not. No scream from you, Sama. Just the words, distinct and sharp, staccato, like shrapnel.

"You want to take a premature baby out of the NICU . . ."

"There are hospitals in Jordan—"

". . . uproot our lives . . ."

"Sama, what other choice do we have? I can't return to Boston, and you might be next. We can't wait for you to get deported—"

"Are you mad?!"

There it is. Thunder and sand and winds that could uproot trees and buildings. I can feel you shake through the phone. I can feel half the globe shake between us. The window rattles.

"You want to take us back to Syria?!"

"It doesn't have to be Syria! We can go—"

"We're not going anywhere! *Sami'ni*, Hadi? Not going anywhere! We're staying right here, in Massachusetts. Your wife and son are going to stay right here, waiting for you. Come home—"

"I can't!"

I burst.

The tarmac, LED-lit. The black-on-night silhouettes of the two officers. Their grip on my arms like steel, colder and tighter than the cuffs biting my wrists.

The tears erupt—"I can't come back!"—flow, sear, destroying me.

Outside, a storm of red and stars, anger and terror both, filling the air with dust, the future we painted yellow, the crib, white, I didn't assemble before I left.

"I can't come home!"

I can't breathe. I can't see the sky anymore. The storm has engulfed even the streetlight.

"Samati."

"No! Not Samati! Not yours, Baba's, anyone's! That's exactly why I left Syria. That's why I put an ocean between me and that place!"

"Sama, please listen—"

"Almost seven years, Hadi! You can't uncross such a distance. Not even you can make me do it! I left so no one could tell me how to live, no one could trap me—"

"What the hell do you know about being trapped?! What do you know about suffering, Sama?"

I must stop shouting. I can't. I must silence my brain. I could put a bullet through it. I don't have one. I don't have anything.

"At home, in Douma, they are queuing to fill plastic buckets and bottles from wells because the water was shut off! My own mother has to wait for the neighbor's son to fill a five-gallon jug for her because she's too old to carry it. She's too old to wait for hours in the cold. And he only comes once every few days and doesn't always remember. My mother, Sama. And she doesn't want to bother him, so she tries to make the water last . . ."

"And you want me to take our son there—"

"No! Come to Amman! We'll figure it out when you do. We could go to Beirut, Paris. We could—"

"No!"

SAMA

Hadi, did you hear what I said?"

The silence that follows seems to last forever, like that split second, midfall, infinitely liminal, when ground and sky are equidistant, gravity and lift are equal, pulling in opposite directions.

"I am not leaving the US," I say, lower, slower, to you and to me. "Not without Naseem, not with him. My son is not an alien. He was born here, and it is his right to stay. And I, I earned mine, Hadi."

The air swells over the ocean between us. My words seem to be taking longer and longer to travel through the airwaves.

"My life is here, and I earned it. All these years away from my family, all those winters . . . Everything I did, everything we did, Hadi. We gave up everything for this."

I hear nothing, not even breath.

"I am not leaving."

There are as many different silences as there are moments and feelings. This one sucks the air out of my lungs. In the vacuum, heartbeats.

This is not the silence of a church or mosque, of a library. Of fog. Not the silence before a yes or a no. I'm not waiting for either. I'm not waiting for anything. I'm not waiting anymore. I can't live like this, Hadi, waiting to live.

Some silences speak. This one.

"How?" you ask quietly.

"What?"

"How are you going to do it? How are you going to stop them from arresting you if they start conducting raids on Syrians?"

I see the doors you are showing me, banging, broken down, hinges ripped out in the middle of the night. I see the detention centers. I see the rain glistening on runways, reflecting planes taking off. I have never felt so scared, or so clear.

"I don't know. I don't know how I'm going to do it, and I don't care. I'm staying here with my son. I'm going to give him the most wonderful life. I'll do whatever it takes."

"And if it takes breaking the law?"

"Then the law is wrong, and I'll break the law. I'm going to give Naseem the best care in the best hospital, and then when he's free to leave, I'm going to take him home and give him everything—"

"And his father?"

The silence of a sort of pain, and the rapid motion of wings.

HADI

Suspended, like dust in midair, like the helpless sand outside, flailing and ravaged by the wind. And insignificant, phone still in hand. Nowhereman in his Nowhereland, nowhere to land. And dry. Parched. I need a drink. I need air. I need to get out of here. This room . . . these stained papered walls, so beige.

What if I ram my skull into one, just to give it some red?

I use my fist instead, but sand and stone don't feel pain. *I don't have fifty days to wait, Baba!* I try again, and again, until the beige is red and maroon and my knuckles are split open, bits of flesh flapping, pathetic. The wall remains intact.

I need to leave this room! And go where? A bar? A liquor store? A gas station where I can drink the gas straight out of the hose? I'll pay, of course, with my shiny American credit card. I need my wallet. Oh look! My passport! A man needs a passport.

Exodus. Outside, khamsin. I can hardly see. A *dikkan* around the corner. I stumble in. All he has are the little travel-size bottles of liquor. I am not picky. I buy a bagful of jeweled bottles.

On the sidewalk—where else do the homeless belong?—I unscrew the first, blue. COTE D'AZUR BLUE, says the label. Cruel. The thought outlasts the bottle. Green is next. Then orange. One by one, the little shots of amber, ruby, fire turn into flashes of magnificent burning.

It doesn't last. The bottles don't last. Nothing does. I'm still thirsty. Where do I go? *There is no water in Douma. They shut it off.*

There is no water in my country. This storm is choking me dry. There must be water at the US Embassy. Maybe they'll give me some.

Three p.m. The last visa applicants brush past me, shadows and dust and the promise of America. Twelve million lucky bastards went through Ellis Island. How many lucky *ikhwan sharameet* got shiny new visas today? I want to start a riot, pick a fight, throw rocks, for me, for Baba, for Mama, for every person who didn't. But I don't see any rocks, just dust, thick, everywhere.

The guards are locking up the gate. The guards are leaving. Tomorrow morning there will be a new queue of visa beggars. I want to cry, shout: Yil'aankon! *I don't want your visa! I changed my mind!* No more groveling on sidewalks like a dog. *I don't need your fucking stamp! You're no better than me! No better! Just fucking lucky, with your liberty . . .*

I choke on my spit and sand. Coughing fit. It turns to rasping, desperate laughs. This is hilarious. So devastatingly funny, this nightmare. All of it. Omar, Baba, Mama, Far' Falastin, *sama.* I can't see sky. Sama, Naseem. I bend over, leaning against . . .

A pipe! A water pipe! Rusty brown and spindly, lining the facade behind me. I punch it. *Mal'ouneh*, it doesn't even fight back!

It bursts immediately, soaking my shoes, flooding everything, *sharmouta*, making a fucking mess on a sidewalk in Jordan.

Across the street from the US Embassy, my feet are in the mud, and I have no other shoes. And they have no water in Syria. And Sama, look, it's all here! The water is all here! It's everywhere, Sama. Isn't that the funniest thing?!

There's so much water, everywhere, look! Going wherever it wants, and I . . . am thirsty. Drained. I collapse on the sidewalk.

Water flows around me and I'm jealous of the water. People walk past and I don't think they see me. No one stops. They all see the water. They're all careful to step around it. No one sees a grown man on the sidewalk, slapping his thigh, howling. Maybe I'm laughing. My God, I'm drunk. My God, I'm not drunk enough. Rising, ebbing, howling waves. And the people walk on! Maybe it's because the streets here are full of men crying on sidewalks. Maybe all the streets . . .

A jingle.

I look up, horrified, but the hand that tossed the coins has disappeared. They glisten on the wet concrete, like drops of honey. I pick them up, one by one, hold them up in the dusty air. At least you asked the homeless man in Harvard Square for his name.

What was his name, Sama? It doesn't matter. I put them in my pocket. It doesn't matter . . .

I see it now. It's a terrible truth. *We* don't matter, Sama. Whatever we do will make no difference at all. The borders won't change, the laws, our passports. The world will keep moving, and the people, and the water still gushing out of that pipe, all over . . .

And suddenly, I'm ravenous.

I want water, bread, meat. I stagger to my feet and away, as far and fast away as I can from the embassy.

There it is: freedom! Walking away, even defeated, nowhere to go or be. I'm drunk and it doesn't matter! Veering left and right like I'm at sea. Let others stand in line. I'm hungry. I'm thirsty. I make it down the street and turn the first, filthy right. There's a filthy shawarma stand. I order three. Three large wraps of hummus-drenched bread overflowing with meat, fries, onions. I stuff the first in my mouth. It falls apart in my hands, dribbling with tahini. I wipe it with my sleeve. I'd wipe it with my passport. I swallow—ecstasy—without chewing, the second, third, with the urgency of survival, tasting my dignity, freedom . . .

No credit card. No problem! I hand the man my coins.

"Not enough, *Oustaz*."

The International Union for Conservation of Nature has issued an urgent warning regarding the disappearance of migratory birds across the Middle East and parts of North Africa. Entire populations are being extinguished by conflict, poaching to fund the arms trade, and refugee needs for food and firewood.

In Syria, the critically endangered northern bald ibis, a cultural symbol of abundance, is down to only three couples. In previous years, these birds had been fitted with transmitters and allowed to migrate. Most did not return. The recordings suggest they were hunted or died of famine. It is confirmed they never reached their destinations.

On the sixteenth of February 2017, time stopped for a moment, as it does sometimes, only for a moment, in that blue, silent space, crystalline and liminal, one sometimes sees from the windows of airplanes.

An infinitely minuscule moment. The world did not notice. Only two people, of the billions on Earth, felt the fleeting stillness.

They stood motionless, those two, on either side of the day, of a sunset and sunrise, of their place in the story of her and him. They looked up and saw trillions of stars, all at once, that stilled, then time resumed. And their story unraveled and frayed. Stars separated and drifted.

On the eastern coast of the Mediterranean Sea, the sun descended—topaz, copper, ochre, and cherry—slipping into the water, imbuing, as it did, the horizon with an earthen aura. West of the Atlantic, it would rise from water, lightening dank, inky tourmaline into indigo, then sapphire, warming the shivering air and birds just enough.

The sun, the sky, sunrises and sunsets belong to those coming or going. Those seeking foothold, for whom the sun is compass, map, timekeeper, diary. But what of the unsettled, not in place, but in feeling? The vagrants, homesick in all directions? Where does the sun rise for them? Where does it set?

On the sixteenth of February 2017, Hadi Deeb did not return to his hotel room. The bed was found undisturbed the next morning. The housekeeper only dusted. The morning after, the unclaimed room was cleared of personal items. There were not many. Some clothes in a rucksack. No money or valuables in the pockets. A used metro ticket; Massachusetts Bay Transportation Authority. That was thrown away. Some other documents. The clothes were stored in a lost and found box behind the front desk. They would remain there, worth neither petty theft nor disposal.

The room was vaguely cleaned and promptly let to a Lebanese businessman in transit. The credit card Mr. Deeb had left on file was promptly charged. The bill, unoccupied nights included, was settled, the police not called; the credit card had gone through, after all.

On the sixteenth of February 2017, the police did record a complaint by the owner of a shawarma stand in the Abdoun district. The stranger had not paid. He had fled. The owner of the stand asked to be compensated. He was not. A report was drafted, eventually. Three streets away, someone found a Syrian passport on the ground. It remains unclaimed.

SAMA

One bag for the hospital, two boxes for you. Your entire existence in this apartment fits into two boxes. They seem to swell in the closet. I won't see them when I close it.

The clothes still smelled of you, faintly—orange rind, cedarwood, pepper—or maybe I needed them to, as I buried my face in the scarves, shirts, cardigans, searching for . . . I found old movie stubs, a ticket to the museum, boarding passes, a hotel card, and every card and little note I ever wrote you. You never told me you kept them all.

Every single one of the notes I used to write and slip into your pockets, your shoes, between your shirts. The pile is bulky; it weighs nothing at all. I found a single, still-crimson leaf from the Japanese maple tree in the public garden. I found a receipt for ginger tea and lemon cake from a café on Brattle Street. I found lines I scribbled on napkins and corners of pages ripped from the free magazines people leave on the T, on the back of fliers—from a movie, a poem, something you said or something we saw or heard together. Florilegium. I found pressed flowers too. I found a feather, alone in an envelope. I do not remember saving it.

I found them everywhere. They fell out of books. I found them in drawers, at the back of shelves. I had to scour the entire apartment. You never wrote back. I supposed it wasn't your nature. Still, for a while, I contemplated no longer sending them. You never told me, I never would have thought, you kept every one of them.

I piled them in chronological order. Now they read like a record of us. I placed the last one I wrote on top, the day you left for Amman.

I place the pile of notes in the second box and close the closet door on them and you. In the living room, the orchid has lost its petals. I'll take it out with me and leave it on a random doorstep on a random landing.

My steps echo on the wooden floor. I circumvent a loose board. One last look around. The room looks back. Nothing, not a scratch on the walls. Not a dent or smear in some corner I could touch that would prove you had been here.

You and I had existed. I thought we had a home here. I know we tried to make one, filling the air with our music and cinnamon, coffee, lovemaking. Now the air smells empty. The walls are still here. Windows, floors, furniture, piano. Only we disappeared. Even so, the apartment looks different. Like a summer house in October, and the beach is bare, and the room is dank and drafty, and the clouds outside are mauve and stormy and there are cracks in the ceiling.

Little white orchid, navy-blue duffel bag with my clothes, for a week at least, a pack of salted crackers, the keys. You don't live here anymore and I, I don't belong here.

I breathe easier when I reach the ground floor. Then I see the mailbox, overflowing. That, too, must be purged. I tear one envelope open, another, all the same. Your name is everywhere, jarring:

ATTENTION HADI DEEB: Card Payment Due. ATTENTION: Insufficient Funds. ATTENTION: Card Limit Exceeded. Suspicious activity. Transaction canceled. Card voided. Please contact us or visit your local branch . . . Dear Mr. Deeb, we regret to inform you . . . Dear Mr. Deeb, Dear Hadi . . .

Life does not stop for the missing, the disappeared; those in limbo; the homeless, home-loose, transient; the impermanent, trapped within the walls of clockless waiting rooms. It careens on, like a train, through borders, fences, gates. Soon enough, it will forget, if it ever noticed, you and me. I should move on too. There is a room in a hospital where I should be.

My heart panics at the blue front door, fluttering, chafing in my chest. I force it on. A razor-thin chill slits across my nape as I step out into the street. I tighten my scarf. Too late; the cold slipped in.

Glassy light disappears into snow the color of ash on the pavement. So do my footsteps. Some café windows are already lit against the outside gray, already foggy with the steam of cappuccinos and lattes. I glimpse them in pairs and threes on tables. My fingers are frozen. I hurry on.

I know this street. This stone is loose; I skinned my elbow here, in front of the antique shop with the miniature carousels. I know the Sunday smell around the bakery makes me hungry. I know this ice-cream shop. I know that a street away there is a better one. I know the steps in front of it, on which we licked gelato, kissed . . . last August, only last August? A galaxy of Augusts ago.

I know this street better now than I would the one I grew up on. I know this city better, this country I was not born into. It knows me better, too, than Syria possibly could. Abu Fuad Khooja and his ashta ice-cream cart would not recognize me.

I know this street and don't belong on this street. I don't belong in Syria either. The homesick have, at least, a home to miss, but this . . .

The sky is a shade of lonely, deeply bottomless blue.

The sky never scared me before you left, Hadi. In Damascus, under the eiderdown that smelled of naphthalene and aged magnolia; in my little room in Cambridge, under the thickly feathered quilt; through the window, through the skylight, I could see the sky and stars and they never scared me. I could see the sky through the roof. I could see through roofs and walls and doors and past them and frontiers, and horizons.

I pass a homeless man by the station and try not to look, but he calls:

"Do you have some change, ma'am, so I can get a coffee?"

I want to pretend I didn't hear. I don't want to see him, know him. I want to tell him I have no change and am as adrift as he. I don't have change. I keep walking, into the station, down the escalator, stop in the midst of ellipses of entering, exiting people, and turn around and ride the escalator back up. At a kiosk across the street, coffee and an egg sandwich. I cross back without looking. A panicked honk and screech and curses. The man takes my offering without a word.

He eats his egg sandwich content, wiping yolk or mustard or both on his trousers. No stains. The trousers are as deeply brown as his fingernails. He chews with an open, toothless mouth, its right corner curving up to smile at me, then takes a swig of the coffee.

If he has ever owned anything, he has lost it and, save for the rucksack on his left—brown too—does not seem to need or miss it. My bag is blue. He eats with his eyes closed, wiping his hands on his thighs, rocking back and forth, slowly, as though to music I can't hear. Everyone else in the swirling, teeming crowd around us is in a hurry, desperate to get somewhere. He has nowhere to be.

And I . . . take my bag of clothes, crackers, books, and then the Red Line to Charles/MGH Station.

SAMA

"You look terrible," Dr. Farber says, without looking up from Naseem's charts. "You need to stop sleeping on that couch, Sama. The nurses are starting to think you're homeless."

My fingers are still numb and clumsy from the cold.

"I went home this morn—"

"To get a change of clothes, I know," she says with an eye on the duffel bag. "They say you go every few days."

The nurses, traitors, who bring cupcakes, crosswords, and magazines and bits of gossip every day. They brought blankets and a pillow last week, and since then, it hasn't been so cold in the evenings.

Dr. Farber turns to the incubator.

"And how did you sleep, little Naseem? You aren't too cold, are you? No, it's nice and warm in there. You should see how cold it is outside! Snow everywhere. Do you know what snow is?"

She removes the box's plastic lid. His eyes are open for the occasion.

"You'll see it soon. It's white and cold and it melts. And you can play with it when you're a little older . . . Let me listen to your heart."

Unwrapping her stethoscope, she warms the tip with her hands and breath before touching his chest. She smiles at him. "I can hear your heart." Then she turns to me. "Would you like to listen?"

Heart. Beat.

Faint at first, barely audible, till she adjusts the metal piece, then a sudden avalanche of fluttering wings. *I can hear your heartbeat, Naseem.* I hold my breath, watching his chest rising and falling, air flying in and out. No mask, no tubes. *Keep going,* ya zghir. *Keep going.*

"He's doing well," she says minutes later, closing the transparent box.

"Small but consistent progress. Good boy. Soon we can start thinking of discharge."

I blink, blindsided, blinded like someone blasted with sun. Midday sun, middle-of-July sun, a skyful, a sunflower field of suns spilling through an open window, drenching the room.

". . . no promises, but barring complications . . ."

I shouldn't. I shouldn't bask in it, drink it in like honey-sweetened lemonade. A breeze dances through that open window. I shouldn't let it. I shouldn't let myself hope, begin to fantasize, about a sweaty, sandy beachy afternoon in that July. A little voice that asks, *Ice cream, please?* Naseem will want . . . chocolate and sprinkles, maybe. Sprinkles melting rainbows into a colorful, dripping mess, from a soggy cone . . . I shouldn't.

But then Dr. Farber says, "And look at that, Ms. Zayat: Your son is one month old today."

The twenty-eighth of February. The twenty-eighth!

In the hospital gift shop, two balloons: one white and one blue. One day Naseem will have a sky of multicolored, silk-ribboned balloons.

Two for now, and the only, misplaced birthday card in the display of bright, glittering *Congratulations, Get Well Soons, Condolences*. I pick my card from the panoply of life events and run out.

On the tenth floor, I hurry down the hall, past other rooms, other lives unfolding. Fragments of conversations and the crying of babies drift out of doors. I do not look left or right. Somewhere, a machine beeps. I start and run the remaining distance to 1013, the balloons trailing like frantic kites behind me.

I don't stop till the incubator. Both hands on the plastic wall, my heart and the balloons catch up. My breathing slows.

"Happy birthday. One whole month, *ya zghir . . .*"

I whisper, and for a moment all else stills, even time, even fear. All but the balloons, teasing each other under the vents, dancing. One white and one blue, like clouds. They'd fly away if they could. *Tiri ya tiyara, tiri . . .* One day, Naseem will have a party . . .

*   *   *

The ceiling is covered with white and blue balloons, their silk ribbons trickling down, shimmering afternoon light over people's heads. Everyone is present.

The guests flutter in and out of the dining room, babbling blessings like a brook in April. Relatives, friends, and neighbors, vying for Naseem's attention, bickering for their turn to carry him. He is dressed in a navy-blue sailor's outfit Sama chose to match his eyes, wide open like the child is amazed, or about to laugh.

He does laugh. No one has ever seen a child laugh so much. Hadi is wearing a blue necktie and a gray blazer.

Hadi has just had his third, rich, turmeric-golden square of sfouf and asks Sama if she wants more atayef. She is in a white dress and could not possibly have another bite of anything.

"Save room for the cake!"

Which will be served on fine, white porcelain plates, silver-rimmed. Where are the napkins? Mama rushes to the kitchen. Baba seizes the opportunity to raid the glorious, gloriously unguarded platter of karabeej. Sama catches his eye. She won't tell. Baba winks.

Mama returns. She has outdone herself. The long oak table is overflowing with glistening, peony-pink, mint-green desserts studded with nuts like gems: pistachios and almonds and pine nuts, sprinkled with coconut flakes. The air is syrupy with the scents of warid and orange blossom, and from the kitchen, the warm, peppery smell of yet another round of freshly brewed coffee.

And in the white afternoon light, the stardust shower of wishes everyone recites:

"Happy birthday, ya habibi! Yin'aad 'aleik! *Allah be with you and protect you, my son . . ."*

Wishes upon God, or gods, or stars, pronounced by adults like children, with the faith of children and trust of birds in the winds blowing them on a certain course, hoping, believing, feathered wings wide open . . . and the blue and white balloons teasing one another and dancing . . .

I open my eyes. I shouldn't have done it, let myself return to that dining room in that apartment I abandoned. That party . . . the desserts were too sweet; the wishes, too many to fit on a single cake; the cake, balloons, colors too vivid. The warmth of all those people, the brightness of that light, too stark against the reality of this room now.

Room 1013 now seems both too small and too empty, with its incubator and windowless walls lined with black boxes blinking depthless red, green, blue artificial lights. That horrid, hard vinyl couch. And those two lonely balloons . . .

But I chose this, didn't I? This vaster world so far away from Damascus. *Tiri ya tiyara,* far from those people and that life, with its clutter of belongings I did not want to take, allegiances and roots that got in my flight's way.

I thought I didn't need them, all that weight, but now I feel vaporous, like I am floating in the air. I press the soles of my feet into the ground, pushing down with all my weight, sealing myself to something concrete. I place my hand on the incubator, palm down, flat, fingers extended, willing all the heat in me to cross the plastic wall and into Naseem's rectangular little world. This room is hopelessly cold . . .

"Samati! We were wondering when you would call. Sayde, it's Sama!"

"*Ya to'brini!* Is she with Naseem? Tell her to turn the video on!"

Homesickness swells in my throat like their voices in the room. Their faces on a little screen, I point to a little sleeping boy.

"*Ya habibi! To'borni!* He looks like his mother."

"Not at all, he looks like Hadi! Look at those cheekbones, and his nose . . . Sama, bring the phone—"

I turn the video off.

"What happened? Wafi, what did you do?"

"*Mashi*, Sayde! Samati, we can't see Naseem anymore."

"I can't seem to turn it on again. There must be a problem with the internet connection on your end," I lie.

Sorry, Baba, sorry, Mama. I couldn't take it anymore.

"I'm sorry."

"It's okay, *ya zghireh*," Baba says, his voice older than it was a minute ago. His exhale fills the space between us, pressing against both our chests, I in a shiny, hollow room, he in a pale-yellow house, on a street in a city at war, where I hear his wife shuffle back to the kitchen—

"Your mother is making coffee."

"Did you find any?"

"No, the stores are still out. Yesterday I spent two hours in line, waiting for bread . . ."

—where, before the power goes, she will boil ground chickory mixed with sawdust, which they will drink on the sofa, pretending it is coffee, talking to me, pretending those flashes of images of their grandson they saw were real.

"Samati, are you still there?"

"I'm here." Whatever that means.

"How are you both, Baba? How is the *wad*'?"

"The same. People hungry and desperate. The schools closed again this week. A few days ago, the neighborhood kids broke into the Badrs' apartment. You remember the Badrs. Their son stuttered . . ." And had a crush on me.

"They're in Canada now. The kids broke the lock and were caught jumping on the furniture, playing with broken glass. You can't really blame them . . . There aren't many places where children can play these days."

Doors wide open, locks broken like hearts. Shimmers of plates and windows, catching rainbows like crystals. Black-and-white photographs, spiderwebs, yellow newspapers. At least the house was alive for a while. At least there was laughter. I see weeds peeking between the tiles; moss in the toilet bowls; orange-streaked, purple flowers on vines riding up the walls. A victimless crime. At least there was sun and air for a—

"Someone came in this morning to install a new lock on the door," Baba says. Then he pauses. Casually, he adds, "Hadi's mother called today. We finally heard from him."

"His passport and wallet were stolen in Amman. He couldn't tell his mother where he was. He was calling from a public phone, but he gave her a number she could call . . ."

"What?" I ask stupidly, to buy my flailing thoughts and heartbeat time to land and readjust to this earth whose axis has just shifted.

"He kept asking about you and Naseem. Poor boy. I can't imagine . . . Iman said he wouldn't stop crying on the phone. *Miskeen*, Hadi."

"He could have called and asked me." I sound cross but am not. I am stranded over the Atlantic.

Baba speaks gently: "Would you have answered?"

I hear the cautious thud of the copper *rakweh* on the marble, and the light double trill of the two white coffee cups. Mama pours. Baba resumes:

"I think he feels . . . Sama, the boy has no papers. He's hiding. He knows if he comes back here he'll be arrested."

"Where will he go?" I ask, high-pitched.

From very far away, I hear Mama's voice: "You should call him . . ."

"No!"

The word has an almost physical quality, like a hot bullet shot from the horror of this past month. Renunciation, of Mama's words and what they implied, reaching out to that land and house and power-cut life at the other end of this line. But most of all, of you, Hadi. You. I couldn't breathe when you left. I still cannot. But I already put the notes away, I put your clothes in a box. I cut off every ribbony feeling that still moored me to you. I'm free. I need to teach my lungs once again to trust sky—"I won't call him. I can't . . ."— and return to this world in which I have no place. I don't sleep in that apartment anymore. The silence echoes.

"I have to go," I finally say.

Baba and Mama don't ask where. He asks if I need money; she asks if I ate.

Naseem and me, and the balloons shivering under the flow from the air vents.

The machines beep, and a louder, dull thumping I realize is my own heartbeat.

A light knock at the door startles me.

"May I come in?"

A crisp *c*. Professor Mendelssohn! His voice is low and warm and glowingly familiar. It silences the beeps.

"You look terrible," he says, echoing Dr. Farber. My throat constricts and the room, all of a sudden, looks watery. He lifts laden arms.

"I brought coffee, and more Hungarian pastries. My wife is determined to feed you and the world into rightness."

He sets his wares on the wobbly table by the blue couch and sits, crossing a leg, as serenely as though he were at a sidewalk café in Budapest. Food and drink are not allowed in the NICU.

"Thank you, but . . ." I smell cappuccino, and something flaky, airy, nearly ethereally light . . . And it is too happy and welcome a moment for rules.

"Kifli," he says as he bites one. It looks like a croissant and smells like an old friend, and my stomach rumbles. I sit beside him on the blue couch and reach for my Styrofoam cup. The coffee steams and the moment radiates, magically normal. For a moment we just sit and sip and do not talk. A brief, untethered moment.

In a spartan room, on a spartan couch, we share kifli, two strangers neither home nor not home, in that moment, as luxurious as pedestrian and transient. It ends with the coffees . . . and my third crescent powdered with sugar. Nothing has changed in the room, in the world, but the skin on my cheeks feels less dry and taut, and my back, surprised, encounters that of the couch, and the blue and red and green blinking lights seem less sharply defined.

Professor Mendelssohn brushes a crumb off his impeccable suit, scrutinizes me, then nods like some geophysical sense of order has been restored. Then he asks:

"How are you?"

I tell him. Everything. It spills out of me like water: events and names and alphanumerics, bits of law, executive orders, countries and headlines. So cruel and cruelly coherent. I lay it out on the couch between us, and it looks so absurd, so spectacularly absurd, that I begin to cry.

I cry like children do at injustice, choking on the words *visa* and *separation*. I cry the distance across the ocean, east through Gibraltar, the sea, spread like giant wings to full fathom between here and . . .

"You don't know where he is?"

I cry the emptiness of this room, the crushing weightlessness of the uprooted.

This isn't right! This isn't the story I was told, promised. The dream, to come to America, work hard, become somebody. Become better and larger than who I was and could be in the life I left. A life beyond the walls in Syria, beyond mere existence.

Freedom, that was the deal!

"It isn't fair," I cry.

"We worked so hard to get here! We both gave up so much!"

I realize I am shouting. I am sobbing, again, to this man whose only connection to me is a course taken, almost seven years ago, on comprehensive bird biology. But this is not anger; this is fear, masquerading as fury, spilling out with the tears. Sky-deep terror like gravity turned upside down, sucking the ground from under me.

I clasp my hand over my mouth, mortified at the scene I just made.

"I'm sorry," I say, and through my fingers, try to slow my breathing.

Professor Mendelssohn does not reply. He hands me his hand-kerchief. *Baba's handkerchief.* And the fear returns with stampeding wings.

It beats about my chest, the urgency to be somewhere where that handkerchief makes sense. Where that handkerchief belongs, and I do. But I cannot see that place. I cannot see the sky. He puts his hand on my shoulder, and I want to believe that touch, that everything will be all right, but I can only cry. His hand stays till I am quiet.

His handkerchief is soggy, and I am mortified, but he takes it and folds it neatly and puts it back in his pocket. Then he just sits there, next to me, on the blue vinyl couch, like he is waiting for a train.

"I know," he says. He removes his glasses and inspects them, then puts them down, and somehow, without them between us, he seems to see me better.

"You are very young. I was very young too when I came here. When my mother and I left Budapest, the Soviets were slaughtering people in the streets. My father . . ." He stops. "Well, he wouldn't have left anyway," he says, not bitterly.

His eyes are limpid and clear, and do not belong to an elderly professor, but to a young boy on a steamer.

"We took many trains and boarded in Marseille—those were the last of the ocean liner days. The crossing took forever then, but I was so happy. And my mother, she spent the whole journey up on deck, on the lookout for the Statue of Liberty. She didn't want to miss it."

He smiles, shaking his head.

"She had this dream of America, of me getting an education. Days before we were even close to land, she had me up there with her, describing New York, pointing . . . I wasn't sure what we were trying to see, but I was so excited I actually believed I could see the statue's torch."

He chuckles.

"I was just a boy. The way you see things when you are young . . . When the statue did appear, eventually, I was disappointed. It was so small! But the city . . . New York was . . ."

He searches for the word.

"Big," he finally says.

YARA ZGHEIB

"It was like magic. New, and shiny, so big, like nothing I had ever seen. For the longest time I actually thought that America meant 'big.' In Hungary, everything was old and cramped and didn't work. Budapest was a shot-up mess in those days: bullet holes in everything, rubble everywhere. Here . . ."

A little boy wanders about the big city's streets. Professor Mendelssohn and I watch him. He could be Naseem. I know that feeling of big. I have walked those streets. A dusky sadness coats me, cold and damp. My voice quavers:

"They don't want us here . . ."

He takes a sip of his coffee and pats his lips with a napkin.

"They weren't too keen on us then either. I heard the word 'commie' a lot, and 'kike.' I had to learn what they meant, but I caught on fast. I had to learn English fast too. My mother never really did, and she was never really able to make friends either. It pained her; she was so alive. She loved people. She was called some quite ugly names too."

He sets his glasses back on the ridge of his nose.

"Sometimes I think it was a good thing she never grasped the language. It would have beaten her to death. The immigrant experience—"

The monitors beep. He looks at his watch, then at me.

"But things changed. That is what I wanted to say. Things change. My mother survived because she was doing it for me, and I became a professor."

268

Through the round, gold rims I glimpse the boy, his mother, their suitcase, and the ocean liner carrying hundreds, perhaps thousands, of people and stories, similar and distinct. *Name, sex, date of birth, father, mother. Place . . .*

I am not certain how long we sit there: I, torn in half; he, American, whatever that means or looks like. From our couch, I watch them disembark and go, the myriad identities and paths that could have been mine, if I had been someone different, at a different time, in a different America. One that was not, did not have a reason to be afraid of people like us. I wish there were a window in this room.

Professor Mendelssohn looks at the incubator.

"This is a very young country. I have hope for it. I think it is greater than people think."

I wish there were a little more air in this young and vast and beautiful country. I wish . . . but everyone does, and everyone wants America. Everyone wants to be free.

Professor Mendelssohn puts his empty cup on the table.

"But you are very young too. And the world is very big."

It sways unsteadily.

He continues: "Why don't you?"

I look at him without understanding.

"Why don't I what?"

"Go back."

"To Syria?!"

There are two kifli left. He reaches for one, takes a bite, and pushes the other in my direction.

"To your husband. I don't know where, exactly, or how, but your son's condition is improving, and if all goes well, he'll soon—"

"My son is American!"

"Yes, but the travel ban . . ."

"The travel ban isn't fair!"

I explode again, once again the child in shocked, breathless pain at the rough, crashing contact with an unjust reality, and the cold indifference of the world looking on.

"I know," Mendelssohn says again, but his quiet tone only fans my rage.

"How can you suggest I leave? You, of all people, how dare you? You know! You came here just like me! Except you got the life you wanted!"

He shakes his head.

"No one has the life they want. People make choices."

"You became a citizen! You got your education, your career!"

"That's right, and I also did not become or get many other things. I never saw my father again. I did not attend his funeral. My mother lived in another language and died in a country far from her family and friends . . ."

"Yes, but—"

"I'm not complaining," he said, "and I know my mother had no regrets either. She said it was just"—he searches for the words—"the cost of living. Hmm, it sounds different in Hungarian."

He swallows the last bite, looks at a fine gold watch, and stands up.

"I must return to campus. Good luck with everything, Ms. Zayat."

He walks away, lightly for such a stout man. He pauses briefly to look up at the balloons by the incubator.

Right at the door between Room 1013 and the hallway, the strip of tiles is a deep navy. On either side, in and out, sky blue. I peer out; the floor is quiet. Behind me, only the monitors.

Sugar still dusts my fingertips. My tongue still tastes the kifli. I try not to swallow, to prolong the light sweetness of the encounter a little longer. It made this lonely room less sterile.

It does not take much to alter the texture of a place, just a few words. A few years. The taste of kifli dissolves. Distance dissolves as easily; a blue vinyl couch, two strangers, coffee.

This is a beautiful country, an easy country to be different in. A painful country to be different in. Maybe all countries are. Or maybe it is freedom that is so painful, so unbearably light and painful. Maybe people build walls because—

A siren shrieks. My thoughts stop, paralyzed, my body too, suddenly invertebrate. Only my eyes dart around, over the doors of other rooms, other babies' and their parents'. One light, bulbous and red, flashes above . . .

"Code blue!"

A voice behind me pierces through even the screaming alarm. Footsteps race past me, rubber screeching, scrubs cadaver blue under the neon, fleetingly purple as they cross the threshold under the crimson-red light, into Room 1010, three doors away from Naseem's room. *Someone else's room*, I tell my heart. It does not hear.

It hurls my body forward. I am at the door. The incubator is blasted open, the lid thrown to the floor. The baby's face is blue. No child should ever be that color. Chest, not moving. Mouth dark, like black currant. A twitch, almost imperceptible, of a little finger and almost translucent gray. A shrill sound—the mother—that could shatter a glacier.

"Ma'am! You can't be here!"

No, I cannot, and will never unsee this. CPR on an opalescent chest smaller than the size of my fist, turning mauve where the fingers pound, pound, pound, my God they pound that little chest.

The blanket that had swaddled the baby lies by the lid, on the floor. The same blanket, white and blue. Thick fingers rub, pound, rub. Repeat. Pound and rub with so much force I am sure they are breaking the baby's ribs.

The child is minuscule, naked arms and legs like dragonfly wings. A hand cups the back of a tiny neck so that it doesn't snap.

A mask is placed over the face, covering it entirely. The mask is a dirty white.

A hand holds a pump and forces air in rapid, consistent, forceful bursts. Too strong, too harsh, too brutally inconsistent with the child's faint gasps, in and out. The pumping pauses and I hold my breath. Nothing. Repeat. *Repeat!*

I don't know how long this sequence is repeated, how long it should be, or how such a metric can humanly be set. *Please little one, breathe. Please little heart, come on,* ya zghir . . .

"How long?"

"Fifty-eight seconds."

Fifty-eight seconds. Only fifty-eight seconds. Fifty-eight enormous seconds. I do not know how time can still be measured, how time itself can still be, when every other law of nature is being violated.

"No response to stimulation."

The pumping resumes with renewed, desperate vigor. I watch the baby's chest sucked in and out artificially, while I do nothing, while I can *see* the little fingertips go rigid.

"Ma'am, you cannot be here!"

A hand grabs my elbow. Steel grips my arms and a faceless body fights my lurching and flailing, shouting something I don't hear, my senses far beyond comprehension. I am pushed away from the room that is not mine. The mother's screams follow me, racking me, forever. The mother's screams will never leave me. The last thing I see is the screen on which a green line stretches, like a tightrope.

One enormous moment. Then a beep.

I hear it. The whole world does. The whole world stops, and every star in every galaxy, for that faint sound. A peep. Another follows. Then another, and the next, and the next, from inside Room 1011, someone else's.

Arms catch me as my legs dissolve. We fall to a heap of hoarse, gasping, euphoric sobs on the linoleum. Arms remain locked around me though I am no longer fighting. Just shaking. The red light over the door is no longer flashing.

The ground is a midsummer sky of blue and white. Like Naseem's balloons. Naseem's little white chest, the drum of my son's little heart. It wasn't someone else's baby, else's life, else's fate. All the walls in the world, real and invisible, crumbled in one enormous moment.

*F*or one enormous moment, she saw it: the sky on the first day of the world, when it was borderless. When there were no walls, bars, or fences, no lines between land, air, sea. When it was all still endlessly crystalline, endlessly blue, endless.

When people were people and all people were people, and when two kissed, any two anywhere, stars exploded, for one enormous moment, bathing the world, all of it, in simultaneous sunrise and sunset.

In one enormous moment, in someone else's room, she saw a human story, every human's: beauty and terror, both. Breath, sun, and death, and what it means to be alive. So complicated, and at the same time, so simple. She had forgotten. Through the ceiling, she saw sky, and above it, the only thing that mattered.

Thrust. It swept her up, and she let it. She pushed the arms that held her wide open and ran to her son's room. No trumpets sounded when she entered.

There it was. It was not here, was nowhere, everywhere. It was Hadi and Naseem. It was, like air, anywhere.

It was beyond all seas, all frontiers, all countries, all beliefs. That longing, that pull that had always been there, that was freedom. Free-

*dom that carries birds from the Arctic to Tierra del Fuego. The same
on which those birds fly back when winter is over.*

*Freedom, intoxicating with possibility. Landscapes so rich in color
and smell they sublimate all senses. She cried, joy and gratitude and
hope, the last with urgency, the same that compels migratory birds to
beat their wings. Hope, that absurd, unfounded, only human capacity
to believe, against all reason and all odds, that all would be well.*

An hour later, beyond seas, frontiers, and countries, Hadi Deeb
shouted into the phone: "What did you say?!"

"I said Amman, Beirut, Vienna, Berlin! It doesn't matter! Let's
go to Paris! Let's meet in Istanbul and take the train . . ."

"Sama, have you lost your mind? None of those places will give
us visas!"

"Then we'll go somewhere that will! And if not, I'll meet you at
some border and we'll live in a tent!"

He could not see her face. She was joking, or simply mad.

"We'll have a picnic!"

Simply mad.

"Are you listening to yourself?!"

"Look, Hadi! Look at this!"

His phone beeped. She had turned the video on.

"Look at his face! Look at him breathe! Look at his eyes; they're
open! I told you they were blue! Can you see him?"

He could. He could see, and it was impossibly beautiful.

He saw his son, his wife, himself somewhere. Not in a place, but a moment, a flash of present that contained infinity. In suspension, midair, nowhere, over the Atlantic, groundless and directionless. And to his surprise, it didn't scare him.

He saw the cosmic majesty of their randomness, that they existed, the three of them, against all probability and circumstance. Then, the cosmic awareness of their impermanence. He saw the sky over the border, at the threshold of night and day. Liminal, infinitely so, crystalline, every shade of blue, studded with stars he did not have to see. He knew.

There are as many loves as stars, shooting across the sky; over the walls men draw on maps, indifferent to those. Loves and stars and birds go where they want, like air, like a breeze. A skyful of loves. And Venus, goddess of love, mornings and evenings, patron saint of the stateless and transient.

He saw planes ascending, descending.

"Paris, you say?" he said, and heard a burst he thought was tears.

"Paris . . ."

It was air.

Under the sky, somewhere, Hadi Deeb hangs up, and pulls a battered rucksack from under a cot. In it he will pack a toothbrush, a half-empty tube of toothpaste, a half-used bar of olive soap. Socks. Nothing heavy. No cookies. He doesn't have photos. Two sets of underwear. He will put on a khaki coat and light he will go, to join the armies of émigrés and refugees, the gypsies, wanderers, transients, homeless and home-loose. The moved, the removed, and those forever on the move along invisible borders. At one of those, he will wait, scattering crumbs of bread for the birds, if there are any.

Under the same sky, somewhere, Sama Zayat sings *'Alli fo' stouh b'aad* to a small boy, about a timid breeze that will take them over roofs, to a place where there are trees. Plums and apricots and pomegranates. Whose freedom is to dig their roots deep in the ground, searching, hoping, fighting for water and the possibility of birds returning.

He will see them, she promises, and the birds themselves, who choose to lift off, go, to seek and fathom beyond the trees, beyond all seas, all countries. Who go, with no promise of land to light on, only a feeling. He will know that feeling, one day soon, when they will go, the three of them together, wherever Naseem wants.

Anywhere. They will travel the world, live freely, see, smell, taste new lands, words, spices, breads, wines, suns, and ideas, insatiably, constantly, endlessly amazed. They will live it all with urgency, each other, and the freedom of those whose sky is beyond all borders.

A NOTE FROM THE AUTHOR

The news excerpts included in *No Land to Light On* were inspired by and composed of a conglomerate of actual news reports of the time, including but not limited to:

1 Angela Dewan, "Airlines allow passengers after judge blocks travel ban," CNN, February 4, 2017, https://www.cnn.com/2017/02/04/politics /airlines-airports-trump-travel-ban/index.html.
2 Lisa Rein, Abigail Hauslohner, and Sandhya Somashekhar, "Federal agents conduct immigration enforcement raids in at least six states," *The Washington Post,* February 11, 2017, https://www.washingtonpost.com /national/federal-agents-conduct-sweeping-immigration-enforcement -raids-in-at-least-6-states/2017/02/10/4b9f443a-efc8-11e6-b4ff-ac2 cf509efe5_story.html.

ACKNOWLEDGMENTS

I want to thank:

Papi, for the handkerchief,
Mamy, for the lapis earrings,
Naji, for the gelato and Sintenis's *Daphne*.

Scott, for green orange and mint, the book of haiku, Camus's notebooks, the croissant, and much more.

Leslie, for telling me to write a love story,
Amy, for believing I could, the first, second, tenth time around.

Daniella, for seeing a writer in me and a book in this manuscript, and Kate, Jade, and every person at Atria who made it real.

Martina, for the daffodils,
Jessica, for the tea,
Andrej, for the *New Yorker* login (which I am still using).

Caroline, Joseph, Sara, Hassan, for the tabbouleh and fruits,
Paula, for holding my hand on the eighteenth of March,
and every nurse and doctor and worker on Ellison Thirteen.

ACKNOWLEDGMENTS

Maggie, for the frozen meals,
Katia, for hearing heartbeats.

Merya, Marwan, for crossing the Atlantic,
Merya, for doing it twice.

Najla, for the light, across the street, in your room,
Line, for the Damascus rooftops,
Mohammad, the orchard in Douma.

Joelle, for saving the orchid,
Hiam, for saving the books, the white couch, my posters of Paris.

Claudia, Maya, Amanda, Colette, Emile, Salim, Ghassan, Joe, Samia, Rose, Paul, Corky, Anne, Henri, Jade, Albert.

And the Liberty Hotel.

ABOUT THE AUTHOR

YARA ZGHEIB is the author of the critically acclaimed *The Girls at 17 Swann Street*, which was a *People* pick for best new books and a BookMovement Group Read selection and received rave reviews from the *New York Times Book Review*, *PW*, *Kirkus*, *Booklist*, and *Bustle*. She is a Fulbright scholar with a master's degree in security studies from Georgetown University and a PhD in international affairs and diplomacy from the Centre D'études Diplomatiques et Stratégiques in Paris. She is fluent in English, Arabic, and French; is mediocre in Spanish; and lives on poetry and travel. Learn more at YaraZgheib.com.